Moonpie and Ivy

ALSO BY BARBARA O'CONNOR

Beethoven in Paradise
Me and Rupert Goody

BARBARA O'CONNOR

Moonpie and Ivy

Frances Foster Books
Farrar, Straus and Giroux / New York

Library of Congress Cataloging-in-Publication Data
O'Connor, Barbara.
Moonpie and Ivy / Barbara O'Connor.— 1st ed.
p. cm.
Summary: Twelve-year-old Pearl feels hurt, confused, and unwanted when her
wild, irresponsible mother leaves her with Aunt Ivy in a little country house in
Georgia and then disappears.
ISBN 0-374-35059-0
[1. Mothers and daughters—Fiction. 2. Country life—Georgia—Fiction.
3. Georgia—Fiction. 4. Aunts—Fiction.] I. Title.

PZ7.O217 Mo 2001
[Fic]—dc21

00-27709

For my sister, Linda,
whose Carolina roots are forever
entwined with mine

ACKNOWLEDGMENTS

A special thank-you to all who contributed to this book: my editors, Frances Foster and Elizabeth Mikesell, for wisdom and faith; my agent, Barbara Markowitz, for enthusiasm and honesty; Janet Zade, for efficiency and friendship (and always being on time); my writers group, for kindness and support; Nancy the Pool Girl Farrelly, for telling it like it is and making me laugh; Ann Cameron, my mentor—wise, funny, and firm; Debbie and Molly Helton, for the postcards; Willy, Grady, Murphy, Matty, and Charlie, the gang I love and who love me back; and the good people of the South, for their spirit and character that inspire me. I am blessed.

Moonpie and Ivy

1

Pearl wondered exactly when it was that her mama had gone off the deep end. Was it that day she marched into Pearl's fourth-grade class and gave the teacher what for so bad the police came and took her away? Was it that night she cut her hair off with a Swiss Army knife just to show that so-called boyfriend of hers a thing or two? Or maybe it was just last week, when she told Pearl to pack her things 'cause they were leaving Tallahassee, Florida, never to return.

Pearl didn't know. But her Aunt Ivy seemed fairly sure of herself as she stood on the porch behind Pearl and said, "I hate to tell you this, honey, but your mama's done gone off the deep end."

Pearl squinted, staring down the dirt road, thinking maybe if she stared long enough she'd catch a glimpse of Mama's car coming back. Pearl was sure that any minute now she was going to see clouds of red dust. See Mama's dented-up old car bouncing up the bumpy road toward them.

Pearl jumped when Ivy touched the top of her head.

"Come on in now, sweetheart," Ivy said. "I'll fix us some breakfast."

Pearl leaned forward and squeezed her eyes tighter.

"I think there's a car down there," she said.

Ivy shielded her eyes from the early morning sun and stared down the road.

"Ain't no car coming, Pearl," she said, shaking her head. "Come on in now, honey. Let's eat something." She nudged Pearl. Her hand felt warm through Pearl's thin pajamas.

Pearl didn't move. Maybe Mama just went down to the 7-Eleven to get cigarettes.

"She mention anything about going to get cigarettes?" Pearl asked.

"She was gone when I got up, Pearl."

"She say anything last night after I went to bed?"

Ivy pulled her bathrobe tighter around her and gazed down the road. "It was kind of a surprise, you know, y'all showing up in the middle of the night like that," Ivy said. "I figured we'd have plenty of time to

4

talk later. Figured Ruby'd explain herself after a good night's sleep." Ivy shifted from one foot to the other, making the old wooden porch creak. "I guess I should've known better."

Ivy sighed. Pearl heard the screen door slam behind her. In the distance, a dog barked. From somewhere nearby, chickens squawked. Pearl wondered if they were Ivy's chickens. The smell of bacon drifted through the open door, and Pearl realized she hadn't eaten since yesterday.

"This'll tide you over till we get to your Aunt Ivy's," Ruby had said, tossing a bag of potato chips into Pearl's lap. "That Ivy, she sure can cook," she had said. "You're just gonna love her, Pearl. You wait and see."

Pearl kept her eyes on the road. The dog barked again. Suddenly a chicken ran across the front yard, wings flapping furiously. Pearl jumped up onto the porch and watched the chicken disappear around the side of the house. Pearl wondered if this was a farm. Must be a farm if there's chickens.

She went inside. Ivy was taking biscuits out of the oven.

"This a farm?" Pearl asked.

Ivy chuckled. "Used to be, long time ago. Not much of one now, though. A coop full of mangy chickens and some dried-up ole peach trees." She heaped scrambled eggs onto a plate. "I had a couple of goats a while back, but they didn't do nothing but look sorry. I give 'em to Nate Collins up the road."

Pearl's stomach rumbled. She eyed the steaming eggs.

"Go on." Ivy gestured toward the table. "Eat up."

Pearl dropped into a chair and grabbed a biscuit in one hand and shoveled eggs into her mouth with the other. The eggs were perfect. Not runny like Ruby's.

Ivy sat across from Pearl, sipping coffee.

"You all drive all the way up here from Florida?"

Pearl nodded.

"Whereabouts in Florida?"

Pearl swallowed a mouthful of biscuit. "Tallahassee."

"Tallahassee," Ivy repeated. "Well, the woman gets around, don't she?"

Pearl looked up. "What woman?"

"Your mama."

Pearl shrugged. Yeah, her mama gets around, but she didn't see where it was any of Ivy's business.

"How long you been in Florida?" Ivy asked.

Pearl sat back and looked at Ivy. "I thought you was her sister."

"I am."

"Then how come you don't know nothing?"

Ivy chuckled again. "Well, I reckon that's a fair

question." She pushed the plate of biscuits toward Pearl. Pearl took another one.

"Ruby and I ain't seen each other in a long time, Pearl."

"How come?"

"Your mama hightailed it out of here as soon as she had the chance and didn't never look back," Ivy said. "Sent home a Christmas card a couple of times. Even sent me a picture of you once, when you was a baby."

Pearl looked up from her plate. "She did?"

Ivy smiled. Her eyes crinkled up at the corners. Just like Mama's, Pearl thought.

"Your granddaddy liked to cried his eyes out at the sight of that picture," Ivy said.

"How come?"

Ivy scraped eggs out of the pan into a bowl on the floor. Two cats appeared from the front room and licked the plate clean.

"I bet Ruby'll be back soon," Ivy said. "Y'all got in so late last night. Maybe she wanted to check out things in town. I expect it's changed a lot since she was here. Why don't you get dressed and we'll go feed the chickens while we wait."

"Mama told me she didn't have a daddy 'cause he died when she was a baby," Pearl said. "But I knew she was lying, 'cause she always lies."

Ivy's face dropped. The corners of her mouth twitched as she fixed a smile on her face.

"Well now, why don't that surprise me?" Her voice was different now. Pearl squirmed a little and wished she had kept quiet. She pushed her empty plate away from her and tossed a piece of bacon into the cat bowl. In her head, she heard Ruby's voice: "Well, for heaven's sake, Pearl, where are your manners? Can you say, 'Thank you'?" But Pearl didn't say anything. She smiled, feeling like she had put one over on Ruby.

She went back to the bedroom and looked at the side of the bed where Ruby had slept. The pillow was still mashed down where her head had been. Pearl leaned down and sniffed. Shalimar cologne. Pearl jammed her fist into the pillow.

She looked around the room. No shopping bags stuffed with clothes and shoes. No red vinyl purse jammed with makeup. Pearl looked on the dresser. No curling iron. No cigarettes. Pearl pulled back the curtain in the corner of the room to reveal a tiny cubicle where a few pieces of clothing hung. Overalls. A raincoat. Pearl squinted into the darkness, examining the floor. A box of Christmas ornaments. A dusty stack of *National Geographic*s.

Pearl sat on the bed. Okay. So here's the situation, she said to herself. No sign of Mama. Not one blessed sign in this dern little room but a mashed-in, smelly ole pillow.

Pearl took a shoebox out of her duffel bag and dumped postcards onto the bed. One hundred and thirty-one of them. She had counted twice. The man at the flea market had let her have all of them for two dollars, including the box and a paper bag full of ballpoint pens.

Pearl lined up the postcards on the bed. All the mountain scenes together. All the beach scenes together. The animals in one corner. People in the other. Then she chose one. The Blue Ridge Parkway.

She took out a ballpoint pen and wrote:

Dear Mama,
I hate you.
Love,
Pearl

2

Pearl held her hands over her ears, making Ivy's voice fade. Only pieces of Ivy's conversation made their way to Pearl.

". . . showed up out of nowhere . . .

". . . after all these years . . .

". . . just takes off during the night . . ."

At that, Pearl took her hands away from her ears and heard loud and clear, ". . . leaving that poor child."

Pearl stared at the wall that separated her from Ivy, imagining Ivy huddled in front of the phone that hung on the greasy kitchen wall. Pearl could tell that Ivy was trying hard to keep her voice low but something about Ruby seemed to stir her up so bad that talking low was impossible.

Pearl went out on the porch and gazed down the road again. Nothing. Just a long, straight road that looked to Pearl like the road to nowhere. A road not even paved. A road with ditches along both sides. A road with potholes full of muddy water.

It had been dark when she and Ruby had driven down this road the night before, so Pearl hadn't seen the clusters of tired old mailboxes leaning against each other or the little houses scattered here and there. Barking dogs and rusty swing sets in the dirt yards. Pearl figured there ought to be some kids around somewhere, seeing as how it was summer, but she didn't see any. Didn't see much of anybody, for that matter.

Ruby had made Darwood, Georgia, sound like heaven on earth. Lied again, thought Pearl.

Ivy came out onto the porch, wiping her hands on her apron. "There now," she said. "I made arrangements for Genevieve to take my place at the diner today so I can stay here with you." She grinned at Pearl.

"What diner?" Pearl asked.

"Diner where I work."

"What kind of diner?"

"Oh, just a little ole diner. Ain't nothing fancy. Open for breakfast and lunch is all. But I sure do enjoy it. I worked in car insurance for fifteen years till my friend Genevieve got the idea to open the diner and asked me to work there. Actually, nagged me dern near to death is more like it." Ivy laughed. "I decided to just take a walk on the wild side and do it." Ivy picked brown leaves off the geranium hanging on the porch. "Sure beats the heck out of listening to people gripe about paying for car insurance all day. Besides, nothing I like better than cooking. Might as well get paid for it. Right?"

Ivy took her apron off and put her arm around Pearl. Pearl moved away. Ivy fiddled with the damp wisps of hair that curled around her face.

"But that's enough about me," she said. "What about you, Miss Pearl?"

"What about me?"

"Well, I mean, what do you like to do?"

Pearl started to say, "I don't like nothing," but something about Ivy standing there grinning and picking brown leaves made her change her mind.

"I don't know," she said.

"Don't know?" Ivy squealed. "Now, how can that be?"

Pearl looked out at Ivy's yard. More dirt than grass.

No trees. A few scraggly old shrubs. A couple of dried-up marigolds in plastic pots. It looked to Pearl like Georgia was as hot and dry and ugly as Florida.

Ivy sat in the lawn chair on the porch and held her bare feet straight out in front of her. She wiggled her toes. Like a kid would do, Pearl thought. Like Mama would do.

"I bet you like boys," Ivy said.

Pearl shook her head.

"Lord, when your mama was your age, she was chasing boys right and left." Ivy held her hair up and fanned her neck with her other hand.

"I'm only twelve," Pearl said.

"I know." Ivy winked. Pearl frowned out at the miserable yard.

"I can stay by myself, you know," Pearl said.

"I'm sure you can, sweetheart," Ivy said. "I bet you've had a lot of practice doing that."

Pearl felt the heat rise up her neck and into her face. She jumped off the porch and ran around to the back of the house. Chickens scurried in every direction. She walked in circles, kicking at the ground in front of her, sending puffs of red dust and gravel into the air.

Pearl stopped at the sound of Ivy's voice behind her.

"I'm sorry," Ivy said. "I shouldn't have said that."

13

Pearl shrugged. She gazed out at the fields behind the house. Bare, stunted peach trees popped up out of the weeds every now and then.

"I can sure see why Mama was itching to get out of here," Pearl said.

Ivy's face twitched a little and she set her mouth tight. There, thought Pearl. Got you back.

Pearl looked down at her hands. The lines of her palms were dark with dirt. She wiped them on her shorts and looked again. The dirt was gone but the lines were still there. She stared at the curved line that ran across the middle of each palm. She could almost feel Ruby's long red fingernail tracing it. "This here's your head line," she had said. "If it's straight, that means you're all squared away and got nothing to worry about. See here how yours swoops down in a curve like this? That means you're liable to be crazy."

That had scared Pearl to death and she had jerked her hand away. Mama had laughed and grabbed Pearl's hand again. Then she had held her own palm next to Pearl's.

"See?" she'd said. "We're the same."

That night, Pearl had lain awake in the dark, praying that in the light of day that line would be straight, but her prayers hadn't been answered.

Pearl was suddenly aware of the silence around her. She looked up. Ivy was gone. Pearl looked out at the dry fields, then to the long stretch of road beyond. Waves of heat rippled in the distance. No cars. No people. No noise. No nothing. Pearl felt all squeezed up inside with loneliness.

She closed her hand into a tight fist and held it to her heart.

"Straighten out, head line. Straighten out," she whispered.

But when she opened her hand, that line was swooping down the same as ever.

3

"Who's that?" Pearl asked, pointing out the kitchen window.

Ivy turned from the sink and craned her neck to look. When she saw the boy in the backyard, her face opened up into a grin. She wiped her hands on her apron and joined Pearl at the window.

"That's Moonpie," she said.

"Moonpie?" Pearl frowned. "What kind of name is that?"

Ivy chuckled. "Well, most folks call him Moon, but that ain't his real name."

"What's his real name?"

"I can't tell."

"Why not?"

"I promised I wouldn't ever tell nobody," Ivy said. "Moonpie's my friend, so I can't break a promise. I leave the telling up to him. Sometimes he tells and sometimes he don't." Ivy put her arm around Pearl and jiggled. She smelled like onions. "I bet he'll tell you, though."

Ivy leaned down and called out the window. "Yoo-hoo!"

The boy looked toward the house. He grinned and waved.

"What's he doing?" Pearl asked.

"Moving my brick pile."

"How come?"

"I was thinking of planting me a bigger tomato garden next year. John Dee says I could probably sell my spaghetti sauce down at the diner."

"Who's John Dee?"

"Oh, just a friend of mine." Ivy blushed. She ducked her head into the open window again and called, "I got them cookies with the kisses in the middle."

The boy threw a brick straight up in the air and let out a whoop. He was inside the back door before Ivy could even put the cookies on the table.

Pearl's mouth dropped open when she laid eyes on that Moonpie boy up close. He was one strange-looking boy. Probably the strangest-looking boy she had seen in all her born days. First off, his skin was so pale she could nearly see right through it. Little blue veins running every which way and freckles sprinkled all over like cinnamon on a cake. And pale orange hair. Like cantaloupe, Pearl thought. But the most peculiar thing was his eyes. Such a light blue they were nearly white, with tiny gold eyelashes that sparkled in the sunlight streaming through the back door. But he didn't seem to know he was peculiar-looking, or else he knew it and just didn't care, because bold as anything he looked Pearl square in the eye and said, "You ever had Ivy's cookies with the kisses in the middle?"

"I never had nothing of Ivy's," Pearl said, studying that pale boy through squinted eyes. "Except some biscuits and eggs," she added under her breath.

"What's your name?" he asked.

"Pearl. What's yours?" She crossed her arms and waited.

"Eugene."

Ivy looked at Pearl and winked. "Told you," she said. She held the plate of cookies out to Moon. He took two. "Pearl's my sister Ruby's daughter," she said, poking the plate at Moon until he took another cookie.

Moon just said, "Oh," and started eating the cookies like they were going to disappear if he didn't eat them fast enough.

"You remember me telling you about my sister, Ruby," Ivy said. Pearl studied Ivy's face to see if she was trying to give Moon a signal. Some kind of sign that said, "You know, my crazy sister, Ruby?" But if she did, Moon didn't seem to pick up on it because all he did was nod and mumble, sending cookie crumbs spewing out of his mouth.

"Pearl might be staying with me for a while. Ain't that right, Pearl?" Ivy said. "Well, I mean, maybe. We ain't exactly sure yet, right, Pearl? I mean, Ruby's liable to come driving up any minute now. You know Ruby." Ivy poked an elbow into Pearl's side, but Pearl couldn't stop staring at Moon. He was taller than Pearl, but that baby face of his made him look younger.

"How old are you?" Pearl asked.

"Eleven."

He stood up and brushed cookie crumbs off his T-shirt onto the floor.

"Nice meeting you," he said, nodding at Pearl. His cantaloupe hair fell into his eyes and he pushed it back. He had this slow-moving way about him that fascinated Pearl. Just blinking his eyes seemed to take a minute or two. Closing them. Holding them shut long enough to show his eyelids, as thin and white as tissue paper and rimmed with sparkly gold lashes. Then opening them to reveal those pale blue eyes again. Something spooky about this boy, Pearl thought.

Suddenly the sound of a car on the road out front broke the silence. Pearl raced to the front door, shoving the screen door open with both hands. But when she reached the porch, the car had disappeared on down the road. Pearl watched the trail of dust fade in the distance. She could feel Moonpie and Ivy behind her.

Don't cry, she told herself. Not in front of Ivy. Not in front of that spooky boy. She blinked hard to keep the tears from coming but it didn't work. She sat on the steps and buried her head in her arms and heard herself sobbing to beat the band. She felt Ivy's arm around her. Then she heard Moon sit next to her and felt his spooky white hand on her shoulder and she wanted to disappear down that dusty road to nowhere.

Pearl cried till she couldn't cry anymore and then she wanted to just lie down right there on the porch and sleep. But she made herself stand up and move toward the door.

"I think I'll go back to my room now," she said. Something about saying those words "my room" made Pearl mad. That little old room wasn't her room. This wasn't her house or her porch or her sister or her friend. Only thing she could put her name on was a dirty duffel bag full of secondhand clothes and a box of postcards.

Pearl sat on the bed and sorted her postcards. She picked one of her favorites. Rows and rows of pine trees, like Christmas tree soldiers. Hundreds of them. She had tried to count them once but gave up. Across the top, in letters formed by twigs, was written: "I'm Pining for You."

Pearl turned the card over and wrote:

Dear Mama,
Please come back.
Love,
Pearl

4

Pearl pushed her face so deep into the pillow she could barely breathe. Then she sniffed as hard as she could. Nothing. Not even the tiniest trace of Shalimar. Pearl had sniffed that pillow every night, and every night the scent had faded a little more. Then one day Ivy had washed the pillowcase and Pearl had thrown such a hissy fit that Ivy had cried.

Pearl rolled over and stared at the ceiling. A jagged crack ran from one corner clear across to the other side. It reminded Pearl of the mountains. She and Ruby had lived in the mountains once. Near Gatlinburg, Tennessee. Pearl had loved it there. Loved the cool, moist air. Loved the woods. Moss growing everywhere like a green carpet. Some man named Howard had taken her and Ruby out to dinner nearly every night. And then they moved.

Pearl could hear Ivy in the kitchen. She got up and looked around for her shorts and T-shirt. She opened the dresser drawer. There they were, folded neatly in the drawer along with the other things she had worn since she'd been there. Pearl snatched them out of the drawer. She put on the shorts and T-shirt and stuffed the other things back into her duffel bag. Then she looked at herself in the mirror. She saw her eyebrows squeezed together in a knot and the corners of her mouth turned down.

"Frown, frown. Turn it upside down," she heard Ruby sing inside her head.

She shuffled down the hall to the kitchen. Ivy was on the phone.

"I'll talk to you later," she said quickly when she saw Pearl. Then she looked down at the floor, blushing, and said, "Same here," before hanging up.

"Now," Ivy said. "What can I fix you this morning, Miss Pearl? I got to go in to work today. I been off too long already. But I'm working the lunch shift, so I don't have to go in for a while."

Pearl shrugged.

"How about pancakes?" Ivy said.

"Okay."

"Moon's going to start digging that tomato garden today."

Pearl flopped into a chair and yawned.

"I just thought you might be glad to have some company, is all," Ivy said. "Gets kind of lonesome out here by yourself."

"I like being by myself," Pearl said.

"Well, lucky is the man who can enjoy his own company, my daddy used to say." Ivy poured pancake batter into the sizzling pan. "Your granddaddy," she added.

"What was his name?"

Ivy stared at Pearl. "What was his name?" She shook her head and flipped a pancake over. "Russell," she said, then clamped her teeth shut and turned back toward the stove.

"Russell what?" Pearl asked.

Ivy whirled around so hard drops of pancake batter flew off the spatula onto the table in front of Pearl.

"Do you mean to tell me Ruby didn't never even tell you her own family's name?" Ivy's neck was splotched with red.

Pearl drew a line through the drops of pancake batter with a butter knife.

Ivy scooped pancakes onto a plate and set them in front of Pearl. Then she pushed a cat off a chair and sat down. "Patterson," she said. "His name was Rus-

24

sell Patterson." She took the top off the syrup bottle and handed it to Pearl. "My mama called him Rusty."

"What happened to her?"

"Oh, some big fancy medical word I can't pronounce and you wouldn't understand anyway," Ivy said. "She died when we was little. Ruby don't even remember her. I'm a lot older than Ruby, you know."

Just then the phone rang, and Pearl's heart dropped into her stomach. There, she thought. That must be Mama. She tried to make her face look calm. Her mind raced to think of what she was going to say when Ruby started crying and carrying on about how she didn't mean to upset everybody and go pack up 'cause she's on her way back. Pearl sat frozen in her chair while Ivy said, "Hello?"

Then she slumped back and dropped her hands in her lap when Ivy said, "But I told Genevieve I was going to work the lunch shift today." Pause. "Oh, keep your shirt on, Jay. I'll be there as soon as I can." She slammed the phone down and untied her apron.

"I got to go in to work, Pearl. They can't do nothing down there without me." Ivy piled dishes in the sink. "There's a bike out in the shed. It's kind of old, but I bet it still works just fine. Have yourself a little tour of Darwood, why don't you?"

Pearl had seen all of Darwood she wanted to see.

"Any malls around here?" she said.

Ivy chuckled. "There's a Belk's down on Route 1. That's about it."

Pearl sat on the couch and listened to Ivy's car disappear down the road. The clock on the kitchen wall seemed to tick louder. A fan whirred in the window beside her. She traced the roses on the couch fabric. Then she got up and wandered around the room. She ran her hands along the tabletops and over the backs of chairs. On the top of the TV she wrote "Ruby" in the dust with her finger, then wiped it off. She opened drawers and peered inside. Looked like Ivy was a saver. Receipts, matchbooks, combs, those little pocket sizes of tissue.

Pearl went down the hall to Ivy's room. The bed wasn't made. A bathrobe lay in a heap on the floor. Over the bed hung a framed, embroidered sign. "Praise the Lord." Pearl went over to the dresser and inspected Ivy's things. A silver mirror with a pearl handle. A tube of lipstick. A hairnet. A pink vinyl jewelry box with "Ivy" written in gold letters. Pearl opened it. A ballerina twirled around to a music box tune. Pearl picked through the jewelry. A charm bracelet, a locket, some hair barrettes. Pearl held up a gold necklace with tiny ballet shoes. She closed her fingers over it and squeezed, pushing the little shoes into her palm. Then she dropped the necklace into her pocket.

She sat on the bed. Her mama had grown up in this house. Had been a little girl in this house. Pearl wondered which bedroom had been hers and Ivy's. She ran her hand along the wall, closed her fingers around the doorknob, touching places Ruby had touched.

Pearl went down the hall to the kitchen and looked out the back door. Moon was in the backyard digging. She was sure she hadn't made a sound, but he stopped digging and looked at her. She backed away from the window and sat at the table.

"Hey, Pearl," Moon called through the screen door.

Pearl sat still, staring at her hands folded on the table in front of her. Maybe he would go away.

The screen door opened.

"Pearl?" He stepped inside.

Pearl looked up. There he was, looking just as peculiar as before. That cantaloupe hair flopped down over those tissue-paper eyelids. He pushed his hair back, and for the first time Pearl noticed he didn't have eyebrows. Maybe a few little gold hairs, but that was all.

"Where's Belk's?" Pearl asked.

"Belk's?"

"Yeah, Belk's."

"Why you want to go to Belk's?"

27

"What else am I supposed to do?"

Moon didn't answer.

"What are you doing?" Pearl asked.

"Digging a garden for Ivy."

"You like doing all that work?"

"I don't mind it." Moon wiped his face with the bottom of his T-shirt. His stomach was even whiter than the rest of him.

"You get paid for doing that stuff?" Pearl asked.

"Sometimes."

"Shoot, you're crazy," Pearl said. "I wouldn't do none of that if I didn't get paid."

"Ivy helps me with Mama Nell," Moon said.

"Who's that?"

"My grandma."

Pearl sat up.

"Where's she?" she asked.

Moon lifted his invisible eyebrows in surprise. "At my house."

"Where's that?"

"Up there." Moon threw a hand toward the backyard. Pearl looked out the window. Beyond the withered-up peach orchard, a wooded hill rose in the distance.

"Up on that hill?" she asked.

"Yeah. Well, back a ways up there." Moon stooped

to scratch a cat behind the ears. It purred and rubbed its head against Moon's dirty knees.

"Why does your grandma need help?" Pearl asked.

" 'Cause she's old." The other cat joined the first one, and Moon scratched it with his other hand. He stood up and wiped his face with his T-shirt again.

"Can't your mama help her?" Pearl asked.

"No."

"Why not?"

"She don't live around here."

Pearl sat up straighter. "Where does she live?"

"Macon."

"What's she doing living in Macon?"

Moon shrugged. "Just living, I reckon."

Pearl pressed her lips together and took a deep breath. This boy sure could be aggravating.

"I mean why don't she live with you?" she snapped.

Moon shifted from one foot to the other and watched the cats. "Some social worker people come out to the house and said she can't take care of me," he said.

"Why not?"

Moon shrugged again. "Just ain't too good at taking care of kids, I guess."

"How many kids has she got?"

"My brother lives over in Lavonia."

Pearl could see Moon was getting tired of answering her questions, but she kept on. "With who?" she asked.

"I don't know. He's grown. I ain't seen him in a while."

"What about your daddy?"

"He ain't around."

"Where's he?"

"Jail," Moon said so low Pearl barely heard him.

"Jail?"

Moon just nodded. Pearl almost said, "What for?" but changed her mind. She wanted all the particulars, and she could see Moonpie was in no mood to give particulars. She'd try again later.

"I got to get back to that digging," he said. "See you."

The screen door slammed behind him. Pearl followed him outside. The backyard was mostly dirt. A chicken coop. A shed. A clothesline. A pitiful-looking vegetable garden.

Moon was drinking from the garden hose. Mud splattered up on his legs. The cats ran over and drank from a puddle. Pearl sat on the back steps and watched Moon dig.

"Don't you want to know why I'm here?" she called out.

He kept digging. "Yeah," he said without looking up.

"Then why don't you ask?" He didn't answer, and Pearl stood up and put her hands on her hips. This boy was kind of irritating, she thought.

"You don't talk much, do you?" she said.

Moon kept digging. Sweat rolled down the side of his face and he wiped at it, leaving a dirty smudge. Pearl stomped over to him.

"My mama just up and left." Pearl flung an arm in the direction of the road. "Just perched her butt behind the wheel of that crappy old car and drove away. What do you think of that?"

Moon stopped digging and looked at Pearl in his slow-moving way. "I think that's mean," he said.

Pearl made a little "psh" sound. "You want to know what I think?" she said. "I think I don't really care what she does. That's what I think." She smiled, but her face felt like cold stone. She wanted to grab that shovel out of Moon's hands and bash everything in this miserable backyard. The shed, the clothesline, the brick pile. Maybe even Moon.

She went to the shed and pulled out the bicycle. The handlebars were bent and rusty. One pedal was missing and the chain drooped onto the ground.

Moon came over and knelt beside the bike. He stuck

his tongue out of the corner of his mouth while he put the chain back on. Then he stood up, wiped his greasy hands on his shirt, and went back to his digging.

Pearl rode the bike across the yard and out into the road. It wobbled and squeaked with every turn of the wheels. She watched the road, dodging holes and rocks. Each time she passed a house, she looked up. Sometimes someone sat on a porch or stood in a yard and stared back at her with a blank face. When she got to the end, where the road met the busy highway, she stopped and got off the bike. A grasshopper jumped in the dry grass beside her. Every now and then a car passed. The strangers inside stared out at her. One woman smiled, but Pearl didn't smile back.

She got on the bike and rode back toward Ivy's house. She rode around the house to the shed, got off, and let the bike fall in the dirt yard. Moon looked up, then went back to digging.

Pearl sat on the steps and watched him work. This boy was spooky. This boy was peculiar-looking. But at least this boy had a face she knew.

5

"We need to talk," Ivy said.

Pearl held the button on the remote control and watched the channels flip from one to the other. She jumped when Ivy snatched it out of her hand. The TV stopped on a soap opera. A beautiful woman in an evening gown slapped a man in a tuxedo. Smack. Right across the face.

Ivy turned the TV off. Pearl stared at the black screen.

"Pearl?" Ivy stuck her face in front of Pearl's. "We need to talk."

"Okay." Pearl looked at Ivy and waited. Ivy's forehead wrinkled up and her eyes darted around.

She sighed and dropped her head back on the couch.

"What are we going to do, Pearl?" she said.

Pearl looked at the black TV screen again.

"About what?" she said.

Ivy sat up and put her hand on Pearl's knee. "About you."

Pearl lifted her shoulders and let them drop. She studied Ivy's fingernails, all chipped up and kind of dirty.

"I don't think I've slept a whole night since you been here," Ivy said. "I can't help but think I ought to be doing something but, I swear, I don't know what to do." Her chin quivered. Pearl sat still, waiting.

"John Dee says I ought to call the police . . . you know, in case Ruby's sick or hurt or something," Ivy said. "He says that's probably why she ain't come back to get you. But he don't know Ruby like you and I do, does he?"

Pearl shook her head.

"Do you think Ruby ain't come back 'cause she's sick or hurt or something?" Ivy asked.

Pearl shook her head again. She felt Ivy's arm around her shoulder. Felt herself being pulled close to Ivy. Felt Ivy's hand brushing the hair out of her eyes.

Ivy sighed again. "Me neither," she said.

They sat like that for a while, Ivy stroking Pearl's

hair, Pearl keeping her head on Ivy's bony shoulder, smelling her bacon-grease smell.

"I was thinking maybe we ought to call your daddy," Ivy said.

Pearl froze. She squeezed her eyes closed and prayed for Ivy to just be quiet.

"I mean, I don't even know the man," Ivy said, "but I feel sure he'd want to know about this, don't you?"

Pearl looked down at the floor. She could see a marble under the TV and wondered where it came from. Moonpie, maybe. Or maybe Mama as a little girl. Maybe that marble had been there for years.

Ivy jiggled Pearl's shoulder. "Well, what do you think?" she said.

"I don't know where he is," Pearl said.

Ivy's face dropped. "Oh," was all she said.

"Mama knows where he is, but she says she don't," Pearl said, keeping her eyes on that marble. "I hear her on the phone trying to get money from him. She must think I'm stupid."

"Ruby thinks everybody's stupid but her." Ivy's voice got all tensed up and edgy. "Thinks nobody's got any feelings but her. Thinks she can just prance around doing whatever she pleases and it don't matter one little bit." Ivy swiped at a tear. She fumbled in her pocket and pulled out a tissue. "She ain't changed a bit since the day she was born. Me, me, me—that's all she's ever cared about." Ivy blew her nose.

Pearl wanted to agree. Wanted to nod and say, "Yeah . . . me, me, me." But all she could do was sit there looking at that marble and feeling a lump in her throat so big she could hardly swallow.

Ivy slapped Pearl's knee and stood up. "Well, I guess there ain't much we can do but wait."

She sat back down and put her hand on Pearl's knee again. "I like having you here," she said.

Pearl sat up straighter and looked at Ivy. In her head, she said, "You do?" but she didn't say anything out loud.

Ivy started into the kitchen. "You like sloppy joes?" she called over her shoulder.

"Yes, ma'am, I do," Pearl said. She hoped her voice sounded polite and thankful, like the voice of someone nice to have around.

Ivy stopped in the doorway. She turned and smiled at Pearl before disappearing into the kitchen.

Pearl got down on her knees and reached up under the TV for the marble. Then she went back to the bedroom and took out her box of postcards. She dropped the marble inside, then dug through the postcards until she found the one she wanted—the Starlite Motel, Interstate 85, Spartanburg, South Carolina. There was a swimming pool in front, the bright blue water sparkling in the sun. People lounged nearby in lawn chairs, smiling, happy to be relaxing on their vacation. Mama loved motels. She'd run around the room messing everything up and say, "There! Let the maid clean *that* up." The next day they'd leave with a new supply of towels and tiny bars of soap.

Pearl sat on the bed and wrote:

> *Dear Mama,*
> *Please come back—*
> *but if you can't come*
> *right away, that's okay.*
> *Love,*
> *Pearl*

6

When Pearl saw Moonpie walking up the road toward the house, she called out, "Hey." He looked up.

"Hey," he called back. He kept both hands in his pockets and kicked a soda can along the ground in front of him.

"Where you going?" Pearl asked.

"Nowhere."

Pearl jumped off the porch and walked beside him.

"Ivy at work?" he asked.

Pearl nodded. In the bright sun, Moon's skin looked whiter than ever. His invisible eyebrows were squeezed together and his spooky blue eyes stared at the ground.

"What's the matter?" she asked.

He sat on the side of the road in the dirt and rocks. Pearl looked down at him. His white scalp showed through his thin cantaloupe hair.

"Mama Nell's looking bad today," he said. He picked up a piece of gravel and tossed it into the ditch. It hit the muddy water. Kerplunk.

"What's wrong with her?" Pearl picked up a piece of gravel and tossed it into the ditch, too.

"Just looks bad," Moon said.

A car passed them. Moon looked up and flopped his hand in a halfhearted wave. A boy leaned out the back window and called out, "M-o-o-o-o-npie," drawing out the "Moooo" part like a cow. Pearl glared after the car.

Moon stood up and brushed the dirt off the seat of his shorts.

"See you later," he said.

"Where you going?" Pearl called after him.

He didn't answer. Pearl watched him walk away. This boy is some kind of strange, she thought.

He turned the corner just beyond Ivy's house and headed up the narrow road that curved up the hill behind the old peach orchard. Pearl ran around to the back of the house. She could see Moon trudging up the hill. She ran to the other side of the shed to see if she could get a better view. She caught one more glimpse of him before he disappeared around a corner.

Pearl pushed through the weeds and briers until she reached the road. She jumped over a gully and landed on her hands and knees. She brushed the dirt off her knees and looked around. It didn't seem to Pearl like a car had driven here in years. Wasn't really even a road. Just two rutted tracks with weeds growing up the middle. Pearl walked up the hill a ways, then turned and looked back. She could see Ivy's house below, chickens strutting around the yard, the freshly dug dirt of the new tomato garden. She looked up in the direction Moon had gone, then back down at Ivy's house. Then she continued on up the hill.

The road ended in a clearing at the top. When Pearl saw Moon's house, she stopped. It looked to Pearl like all that house needed was a gust of wind to send it tumbling down the hill in a heap of splintered wood. Two tiny windows. No screen on one and a screen full of holes on the other. The front porch was a piece of rotten plywood on cinder blocks. Plants in rusty coffee cans lined the edges. The house was a moldy green color, the bottom half stained orange from the redorange dirt of the yard.

Pearl stood still and listened. Nothing. Just the buzzing of flies and the muted sound of a radio from somewhere inside.

Pearl wanted to make herself turn around and go home. Mind her own business for a change. But instead she tiptoed to the house and crouched beneath a window. She heard Moon say something. Heard a gravelly voice say something back. She rose slowly until she could see over the windowsill. It was dark inside. She squinted and pressed her face against the dirty screen.

The floor of the dark little room was littered with piles of clothes and stacks of newspapers. Dishes, cardboard boxes, and paper bags. Moon sat by a bed piled with blankets. Pearl could tell somebody was in the bed, but all that was showing was a wrinkled-up face and tufts of white hair poking out in every direction.

A stale, medicine smell hung in the air. Pearl wrinkled her nose and ducked back down. She started to leave, but stopped when she heard Moon's voice. She sat still, listening. Moon was reading from the Bible. Pearl didn't know much about churchgoing, but she knew Bible words when she heard them.

When Moon stopped reading and the room was quiet, Pearl raised up slightly and peered in the window again. Moon was kneeling by the bed, his head on the pillow next to that wrinkled-up old face. His

41

cantaloupe hair flopped down on top of those tufts of white. Pearl tiptoed away from the house, crouching, then took off running down the hill toward Ivy's.

When she got to Ivy's back porch, Pearl sat on the steps to catch her breath. She put her chin on her knees, thinking. She wondered which was worse—your mama not wanting you and you having nobody else, or your mama not wanting you and the only other person you have is a wrinkled-up old lady in the bed.

Pearl went inside and dialed the number of the diner that Ivy had taped on the wall beside the phone.

Ivy answered. Pearl could hear dishes clattering in the background.

"This is Pearl," she said.

"What's wrong?" Ivy's voice was squeaky and scared-sounding. Pearl had never called the diner before.

"Nothing."

Pearl heard Ivy let her breath out.

"Well, okay," Ivy said. "That's good."

Pearl heard someone holler Ivy's name.

"You need something, Pearl?" Ivy said.

"No."

"You sure you're okay?"

"Yeah."

Dishes clattered again. "Maybe I can come get you

on my break," Ivy said. "You can sit here at the counter and talk to me while I work. I'll fix you a cheeseburger. How about that?"

Pearl felt the tears coming and was glad Ivy couldn't see her. She wiped her nose with the back of her hand. She didn't want to talk. She just wanted to hear Ivy's voice.

"Pearl?" Ivy said.

Pearl sniffed and cleared her throat. "What?"

"You okay?"

Pearl nodded, wiping at the tears. Maybe it was better to have a wrinkled-up old lady in the bed than to have nobody.

"You stay right there. I'm coming home," Ivy said.

"No!" Pearl said louder than she meant to. "I was just wondering what time the mail comes, is all. I expect I'll be hearing from Mama, so I just wanted to know that—about the mail. That's all."

There was silence on the other end of the line. Then Ivy said, "Oh." Someone hollered Ivy's name again. "Well, uh, the mail gets there about noon."

"Okay," Pearl said and hung up.

Pearl sat at the kitchen table, listening to the whir of the window fan. A cat jumped in her lap and she pushed it off.

Then she went back to her bedroom and took out the shoebox. She closed her eyes and picked a postcard. The pink flowers of a dogwood tree. "Beautiful Carolina Dogwood," it said on the back. Pearl flopped on her stomach on the bed and wrote:

> *Dear Mama,*
>   *There's this spooky boy*
> *named Moonpie. His mama is*
> *no good like you but at least he*
> *has somebody else even if it is*
> *a wrinkled-up old lady in the bed.*
>   *Love,*
>   *Pearl*

7

"Pearl, this is John Dee. John Dee, this is Pearl," Ivy said.

John Dee took his greasy baseball cap off and nodded toward Pearl. "Nice to meet you," he said. His voice was raspy, like the voice of someone who smokes too much.

"I told him all about you," Ivy said.

Pearl wondered what that meant. Didn't seem to her like there was much to tell except the bad part. The part about Ruby.

"John Dee's going to take us out for pizza tonight." Ivy smiled up at John Dee. He fiddled with his cap. His arms were thick and hairy. Part of a tattoo showed from under the sleeve of his T-shirt. A snake. Or a dragon, maybe. Pearl couldn't tell which.

"Let's go up and get Moonpie," he said.

Ivy's face lit up. "Well, now that's a good idea. I got to go up there anyhow and check on Mama Nell." She turned to Pearl. "You want to ride up there with us?"

"Okay," Pearl said.

"Let me get some of them chicken and dumplings I got in the freezer," Ivy said. "Y'all go on out and I'll be right there."

Pearl followed John Dee outside. A rusty, dented van with J.D. APPLIANCE REPAIR painted on the side was parked out front.

"That your van?" Pearl asked.

"Yep," he said, opening the door for Pearl.

There were only two seats, so Pearl climbed in back and sat on a plastic milk crate. John Dee sat in the driver's seat, drumming his fingers on the steering wheel.

"What do you think of Darwood?" he asked.

"I don't know." Pearl watched the back of his head. His hair was greasy and hung in clumps. The back of his neck was sunburned.

"Ivy tell you about my mama?" Pearl said.

John Dee kept drumming his fingers on the steering wheel and looking toward the house. "She's told me a bit about Ruby," he said, nodding.

"Like what?"

He took his baseball cap off, scratched his head, and put his cap back on. "Well now, let me think," he said. "Told me Ruby's a lot younger than her. Told me she left Darwood quite a few years ago." He turned and winked at Pearl. "Told me she had a daughter named Pearl," he added.

Pearl leaned forward. "No, I mean, she tell you about her leaving me and all?"

A look of sheer relief flooded over John Dee's face when Ivy came out of the house and opened the door of the van.

"Sorry I took so long," Ivy said, climbing in. "I was hunting for them bread-and-butter pickles Mama Nell likes so much." She held a bag in her lap and looked back at Pearl.

"The doctor tells her not to eat them pickles," Ivy said, "but I say, pooey. Whatever makes her happy, right?"

The van started with a roar and a puff of black smoke. They turned onto the narrow, rutted road leading up to Moonpie's house. Tools rattled and slid from one side of the van to the other as they bounced along. Pearl struggled to keep from falling off the milk crate, and Ivy laughed all the way up like something was hysterical.

When the moldy green house came into view, Pearl

saw Moon out front, throwing darts at the side of the house. When he saw the van, he grinned.

"Hey," he called, running over to the driver's side.

"Hey back at ya," John Dee said.

The van door squeaked when he opened it. "I'm going to have to fix that someday," he said. He and Moon grinned at each other. John Dee jabbed Moon in the side with an elbow. Must be some kind of private joke, Pearl figured. It didn't seem too funny to her, though.

"How's Mama Nell?" Ivy said, gathering up the bag of food.

"She don't look too good," Moon said.

"She eat anything today?"

"Some soup."

"I'll go in and check on her." Ivy started toward the house. Pearl followed her.

"I'll come, too," Pearl said. She was dying to see the inside of that house.

"Naw, now, you stay out here and enjoy the fresh air and sunshine with the boys." Ivy disappeared inside, the screen door banging shut behind her. Pearl could hear her singsongy voice inside calling, "Mama Nell? It's me—Ivy."

When Pearl turned back toward the yard, John Dee and Moonpie were throwing rocks into the woods. Every now and then a loud thwack echoed through the trees.

"How old is she, anyway?" Pearl said, jabbing a thumb in the direction of the house.

"I don't know," Moon said, grunting as he hurled a rock into the woods. "Old."

"Still got plenty of spit and vinegar. I guarantee you that," John Dee said. He searched the ground for another rock.

"Don't look like it to me," Pearl said. She didn't think it was possible, but Moon's white face actually turned red clear down to his neck.

"I reckon it's just the heat is all," Moon said.

"I'm glad you said that," John Dee said, opening the back of the van. "I got a fan for you. Don't look like much, but it works real good." He held up a rusty fan with silver duct tape holding the sides together. "I'll go set this up in there."

When the screen door shut, Pearl turned to Moon.

"So, who's he?" she said. "Some kind of boyfriend?"

She had asked that question of Ivy but hadn't gotten an answer that satisfied her.

Moon shrugged and wiped the back of his neck. He closed his eyes in one of those long blinks, then looked at Pearl and shrugged.

Dern, thought Pearl. Don't nobody want to talk about nothing around here.

Ivy and John Dee came back outside. Ivy shook a rug off the edge of the rotten little porch.

"Moonpie, them flowers are drying up," Ivy said, pointing to a row of drooping sunflowers near the house. "Get that bucket over yonder and let's water 'em."

When the flowers were watered, Ivy put her arm around Moon.

"There," she said. "Now let's go get us some pizza."

"What about Mama Nell?" Moon asked.

"Aw, she's fat and happy and snoring away," Ivy said. "Done eat half a jar of them pickles."

At the restaurant, Pearl didn't feel much like eating. Ivy and John Dee kept smiling at each other, and Ivy would giggle and blush and carry on. Then John Dee kept ruffling Moonpie's hair and they'd be poking each other and cracking jokes that weren't funny and then falling all over themselves laughing. Pearl just sat there feeling like she'd been plunked down in the middle of something that didn't have one little thing to do with her.

Then things got worse when they bounced back up the road to Moonpie's house. Moon sat on a paint bucket between the seats, holding on to the dashboard. When they stopped in front of the house, Moon said, "I was thinking I ought to talk to y'all about something."

Ivy's face got serious. "What?" she said.

Moon looked down at his hands and fiddled with his T-shirt.

"That social worker lady's supposed to come tomorrow," Moon said, "and, well, uh, I was thinking . . ."

"What social worker lady?" Ivy said.

"Aw, some lady supposed to come out and check on us." Moon twisted the bottom of his T-shirt around his finger. "I ain't exactly sure why."

"I thought she just come out a while back." Ivy pushed Moon's hair out of his eyes.

"She did."

"Then why in tarnation is she coming again?"

Moon lifted his shoulders up to his ears and held them there a minute before letting them drop. "I think she's thinking Mama Nell can't take care of me no more," he said in a tiny little voice. Pearl watched his face. Was he going to cry? It looked like a possibility.

Then Ivy just exploded. Made everybody in the van jump.

"Can't take care of you! Ha! Mama Nell's got more brains than all them social workers put together." Ivy sat on the edge of her seat and threw her hands around. "I'd just like to see them come up here and start something. Them social worker types, they all think 'cause they been to college they know it all—

know all about who can take care of who. If they want an education, just let 'em come up here and I'll give 'em one."

John Dee reached over and put his big hairy hand on Ivy's shoulder. "Ain't nobody starting nothing, Ivy," he said real soft. "What you getting all riled up for?"

Ivy crossed her arms and sat back against the seat. "Well, I just don't want nobody trying to change things up here, that's all," she said. Her voice was calmer now. She looked at Moon.

"Why you think that lady thinks that about Mama Nell?" she asked.

"Just a feeling, I reckon," Moon said.

"Anybody ever say anything to you about that?" John Dee asked.

"They was all the time saying it after Mama left," Moon said. "Saying Mama Nell was old and all and how could she take care of me. Stuff like that."

"Ha!" Ivy said, throwing her head back. "They don't know nothing about nothing. Don't you worry about it, Moon." She patted his hand.

"I just thought maybe shouldn't nobody come out here till Mama Nell gets better," Moon said.

"I'll call that lady first thing tomorrow," Ivy said. "Won't nobody be coming up here, okay?"

Moon looked like a little kid, all slumped down with his head hanging. He nodded real slow.

Ivy and John Dee both reached out at the same time and put a hand on Moon's knee. Pearl felt a stab right through her heart that took her by surprise. She watched the three of them, sitting there connected in a way she didn't understand.

She cleared her throat and squirmed on the milk crate, but nobody noticed. She looked at Moonpie, sitting there with his head hanging, and Ivy and John Dee with their hands on his knee and their faces all full of worry.

Shoot, thought Pearl, at least that spooky boy has somebody. She didn't have anybody except a crazy mama who tossed her out like a sack full of stray kittens. It seemed to Pearl like somebody ought to be sending some of their worry her way.

8

"What you wanna do?" Moon asked, running his hand down a cat's back and all the way up its tail.

Pearl was stretched out on the couch with her feet up on the arm. "Ain't nothing *to* do around here," she said. Pearl had been at Ivy's two weeks now, and she figured she'd done about everything there was to do in Darwood, Georgia, which was about two clicks past nothing.

"We could catch crawfish down at the creek."

"Crawfish?" Pearl held her feet in front of the window fan. "Why would we want to do that?"

Moon shrugged. "I don't know," he said. "Something to do."

Pearl swung her legs around and sat up, putting her face in front of the fan. Her bangs blew straight up in the air.

"It's too hot to go outside," she said.

"It's cool down at the creek," Moon said. "There's woods there, and the water's cold."

Pearl slumped against the lumpy couch cushions. She inspected her legs. Too hairy, she thought. Maybe she'd shave them. Ruby had shaved them for her once. Painted her toenails red and bought her some pink plastic sandals. The next day they went to a barbecue in somebody's backyard. There were no other kids there and Pearl had walked around and around the yard in her pink sandals. Ruby had gone off in a car with somebody and hadn't come back until the hamburgers were all gone and everybody was eating ice cream. Pearl had taken off her pink sandals and tossed them under somebody's pickup truck in the driveway.

Pearl jumped when Moon said, "Come on. Let's go down to the creek."

She pushed herself up off the couch and shuffled toward the door. "A creek," she said. "Whoop-dee-doo." She pushed the screen door open with her foot. The cat darted out ahead of them.

Outside, the air was still and thick with heat. Pearl followed Moon through the peach orchard. The back of his shirt was dirty and wet with sweat. He lifted his bony white knees up high as he made his way through the tall weeds.

Every now and then the thorns of a blackberry bush snagged Pearl's T-shirt or scratched her legs. She wished she hadn't worn flip-flops.

"How much farther?" she said, waving gnats away from her face.

"Just over there in them woods." Moon pointed to the line of trees ahead of them.

When they entered the woods, the air was cooler. Ferns lined the path and tickled Pearl's legs. Insects buzzed and lizards scurried through the dry leaves. Pearl liked it here. She wanted to lie down on the mossy ground and look up at the sky through the trees. She had always loved the woods. Loved the smell of the damp earth, the way the trees could fold you in and swallow you up.

They hadn't gone far when Pearl heard the sound of water. She followed Moon through the trees to the edge of a creek. The water was clear and shallow, flowing lazily over moss-covered rocks. Tiny silver minnows darted just below the surface.

Moon picked up a rusty can from the edge of the creek and peered inside. He turned it over and dumped a clump of wet sand out onto the ground.

"We can use this to put the crawfish in," he said.

He walked into the water with his sneakers on and started turning over rocks.

"I'm not going in that water," Pearl said. "I'm going on up that path a ways."

Moon didn't answer as Pearl headed up the path away from the creek. The slap-slapping of her flip-flops echoed in the woods as she walked along. Not far from the creek, a narrow path branched off through a tangle of wild shrubs. Pearl could see sunlight filtering through the trees and wondered if the path led to a clearing. She ducked under low-hanging branches and followed the trail. Sure enough, she hadn't gone far when she came out into an open area.

After the darkness of the woods, it took a minute for her eyes to adjust to the bright sunlight. She squinted. Was she seeing things? Scattered around the clearing were tombstones, nestled among the weeds and wild daisies. Some were cracked and leaning. A few were made of shiny black marble. One had an angel perched on top.

Pearl had never been in a graveyard before. She walked slowly between the graves, reading the names etched on the stones. Bertha May Hayes, Beloved Wife and Mother. Raymond Gerald Patterson, Gone But Not Forgotten.

Some of the graves had little fences around them. Morning glories twined in and out of the rusty gates. Pearl wandered from stone to stone, moving her lips silently as she read. When she reached the far side of the graveyard, she looked up.

"Whoa," she said out loud.

In the middle of the graveyard was a circle of sunflowers. They were taller than Pearl. So yellow against the blue sky they didn't look real. Some of them drooped, hanging their heads like pouting children. Pearl ran over to them and peered up into their flower faces. Then she noticed that in the middle of the sunflower circle were two tiny graves marked with two tiny stones. Pearl knelt and inspected them. Rose Marie Jennings, God's Precious Little Angel, read one. Margaret Jane Jennings, Child of Heaven, read the other.

Pearl ran her hand over the grass in front of the stones. There were *children* buried here. Imagine that! Two little children way down under this grass and dirt. Pearl had a scary, excited feeling in her stomach.

She looked up at the sunflowers, standing guard over the little graves. Then she lay down and stretched out with her head against one of the stones and her feet crossed at the ankles. She placed her hands on her chest and closed her eyes. I am Rose Marie, God's Precious Little Angel, she thought.

"How come there's a graveyard way out here in the woods?" Pearl asked.

"Ivy says it's a family graveyard's been here a long time. Ain't nobody buried here but her kin." Moonpie got up and brushed off the seat of his shorts. "I'm going to go dump them crawfish back in the creek and get on home," he said, then disappeared into the woods.

Pearl looked around her at the gravestones. Ivy's kin? Then these dead people were her kin, too. That sure beat all. She was all the time wishing she had family and now here she had gone and found some and they were all dead.

That night Pearl arranged her postcards on the bed. She closed her eyes and circled her finger over them several times before bringing it down on top of one. She opened her eyes and looked at the postcard under her finger. Table Rock Mountain. She and Ruby and some woman named Eve had had a picnic there once. Ruby and Eve had sat on the hood of the car and drunk warm beer while Pearl played in a creek nearby. They wanted Pearl to drink the warm beer, too, but Pearl had pretended like they were invisible and Ruby had gotten mad and called her a name. What name was it? Pearl couldn't remember.

She turned the postcard over and wrote:

"Get up off of there!" Moon's voice cut through the silence and echoed in the clearing.

Pearl jumped up. "What's wrong with you?" She glared at him. "You tryin' to scare me to death?"

Moon glared back at her. His hair flopped down over his eyes but he didn't brush it away. Just glared right through it.

"You ain't supposed to be on them graves," he said in such a mean voice Pearl was fascinated. Here was sweet little Moonpie, all riled up for a change. She smiled.

"What's the matter? You think Rose Marie is gonna jump up out of that ground and holler at me?" she said.

Moon lunged at her. He shoved with both hands, knocking her clean off her feet and taking the breath out of her.

She scrambled up off the ground. "What's the matter with you?" she yelled, clenching her fists and stepping toward Moon. "Don't you never touch me again or I'll knock your block plumb off!"

Moon's chest heaved and his chin quivered. Then, just as quickly as the mad had swept over him, he seemed to melt right before Pearl's eyes. His shoulders slumped and his face drooped and he sat right down on the ground.

"I'm sorry," he said so low Pearl could barely hear him.

"You better be sorry," she said, standing over him with her fists on her waist.

She waited, but Moon didn't say anything else. She sat beside him on the grass and waited some more. Still nothing.

"You mind telling me why you went and acted like a crazy person just 'cause I was laying there on a grave?" Pearl said.

Still nothing. She pushed Moon's shoulder.

"I'm talking to you!" she yelled in his ear.

Moon turned his head slowly and looked at her. He blinked one of those slow-motion blinks. His gold eyelashes practically shimmered in the sunlight. Pearl could feel herself getting all churned up with irritation.

"Them graves are Ivy's babies," Moon finally said.

"Ivy's!" Pearl looked over at the sunflower circle and the two little gravestones, then back at Moon.

"Ivy had babies?" she said.

Moon nodded.

"And they died?"

Moon nodded again.

"When?"

Moon pulled at a blade of grass and flicked it into the air. "A long time ago," he said. "Before I was born."

"What happened to 'em?"

"Born dead."

Pearl shook her head and said, "Wow."

They sat there in the graveyard in silence. Pearl watched a butterfly flutter around among the graves.

"But Ivy ain't married," she said so loud and sudden that Moon jumped.

"Used to be," he said.

"Then where's her husband?"

"They got divorced."

"Well, what do you know," Pearl said. "I sure never would've guessed that."

"Didn't your mama never tell you nothing about Ivy?" Moon said.

"She never told me nothing about nothing," Pearl said. "Except big fat lies," she added.

Moon put his chin on his knees and closed his eyes. "Ivy comes here a lot," he said. "I seen her have a picnic here once, all by herself."

"Really?"

"I was down at the creek and I could hear her talking but wasn't nobody here." Moon nodded toward the sunflower circle. "She waters them sunflowers, too. Hauls water up from the creek in a bucket."

Dear Mama,

Did you know Ivy had babies that died? They are buried with all our kin in a circle of sunflowers. When I die, you can bury me there and call me God's Precious Little Angel Child of Heaven. I bet you'll be sorry then.

Love,

Pearl

9

"I swear, Mama Nell's looking worse every day," Ivy said, snapping the ends off a green bean and tossing it into a bowl.

Pearl watched Ivy's hands. Her fingers were long and thin and covered with freckles. There was dirt under her fingernails from weeding the tomato garden.

Ivy sighed and shook her head. "I don't know how much longer I can keep them social workers away," she said.

"Why do you need to keep them away?" Pearl asked. She reached for a bean and snapped the ends off the same way Ivy did.

Ivy stopped her snapping and gave Pearl a surprised stare. " 'Cause of Moonpie, that's why."

"Why 'cause of Moonpie?"

Ivy leaned closer to Pearl. "Well, what in the world would happen to him if them high-and-mighty people took a notion that Mama Nell can't take care of him?"

"Seems to me like he's the one taking care of her," Pearl said.

Ivy snapped a bean and threw it in the bowl so hard it bounced right back out onto the table.

"She's just having a bad spell, is all," Ivy said. "That woman can run circles around them social workers any day of the week, and that's a fact."

Ivy's freckled neck was getting those red splotches again. Pearl shrugged and said, "Whatever."

Ivy set her lips together tight and breathed out hard through her nose.

"Why don't his mama come get him?" Pearl said.

"That no-account piece of nothing?" Ivy snapped and tossed. Snapped and tossed. "She oughtta be horse-whipped for not taking care of that child."

"Where'd she go?"

"Who knows. Last I heard, she was running wild over in Macon." Ivy's face got redder. "Makes my blood boil," she said.

They sat in silence for a while, snapping and tossing

beans. Pearl could tell Ivy was all worked up about something, the way her splotchy neck got redder and her fingers snapped those beans so fast.

"Don't take care of her own child," Ivy said. "God gives a woman the greatest gift on earth and she just throws it away like yesterday's garbage."

"Maybe some women don't look at things the same as you," Pearl said. "Maybe some women think their kids *are* yesterday's garbage."

Ivy put her hand to her mouth. "Oh, honey, I'm sorry. What in the world was I thinking talking to you like that?"

She came over and put her arms around Pearl. Her skin was warm and damp. Pearl breathed in the earthy smell of her.

Ivy took Pearl's shoulders in both her hands and gave her a little shake.

"Don't you listen to me, you hear? Sometimes I just spout off all kinds of nonsense. It's a wonder somebody don't haul me off to the noodle farm." She smiled and pushed Pearl's bangs off her forehead.

Pearl wanted to be little again. She wanted to curl up in Ivy's lap and say, "Tell me I'm the greatest gift on earth."

And then the phone rang and Pearl got that instant knot in her stomach. Now *that* must be Mama, she thought. Maybe she'd tell Ruby not to come back for a while. Maybe not for a week or two anyway. Give them both a little break from each other.

Pearl waited while Ivy said, "Hello?" She watched Ivy's face and her heart beat so hard she thought surely Ivy could see it jumping around under her T-shirt.

"I don't know, hon," Ivy said into the phone. "I hate to leave Mama Nell alone that long."

Pearl's heart settled back down to normal again. She tossed a bean into the bowl and went back to the bedroom. She took out her shoebox and sat on the bed. She fished around through the postcards until she found the ballet shoe necklace. She held it up and watched the little shoes swing back and forth. Every now and then, she could hear Ivy's voice drift down the hall from the kitchen. "Moonpie . . . Moonpie . . . Moonpie." It seemed like all Ivy ever talked about was Moonpie. Seemed like all she *cared* about was Moonpie. What about Pearl? Wasn't she the greatest gift, too? Maybe not. Maybe she really was yesterday's garbage.

When she heard Ivy's footsteps in the hall, Pearl dropped the necklace back in the shoebox. She slammed the lid on just as Ivy stopped outside the door.

"Me and John Dee were thinking about going up to Moon's to play Yahtzee," Ivy said. "You wanna go?"

"Nah." Pearl stared out the window, setting her face into a don't-bother-me-I'm-not-interested look.

"How come?" Ivy sat on the bed beside Pearl. Pearl put both arms over the shoebox.

"Just not interested," she said.

Ivy glanced at the shoebox. Pearl stared out the window.

"If you change your mind, come on up," Ivy said.

Pearl pushed aside the faded curtains and watched Ivy and John Dee trudge through the weeds, jump over the ditch, and disappear up the dirt road toward Moon's house. She flopped back on the bed and looked up at that crack in the ceiling. She could hear the chickens shuffling around out in the yard.

She slipped on her flip-flops and went out on the back porch. She looked in the direction of Moon's house and wondered what they were doing up there. Wondered if they were all laughing, slapping each other on the back, maybe even hugging every now and then. She bet Ivy and John Dee were making a fuss over Moonpie. Telling him he was the world's best Yahtzee player and all. That old woman, Mama Nell, was probably just laying there taking it all in. Maybe they'd take a break and have some of Ivy's cookies with the kisses in the middle. They'd sit on the porch and eat their cookies. Just one big happy family.

Pearl crossed the yard to the tomato garden. She pulled a green tomato off one of the plants and threw it as far as she could out into the peach orchard. She heard it land with a thud somewhere in the weeds.

She shuffled around the dirt yard, kicking rocks and leaving a trail of red dust behind her. She ran her hand along the wet sheets hanging on the clothesline. A chicken clucked along in front of her, pecking at pebbles in the dirt. Pearl flapped her hands to shoo it away, then noticed something in the cement that held the clothesline pole in the ground. She knelt and examined it. A handprint. Above it, the name "Ruby" carved in big, wiggly letters. Pearl stared at it. She reached her hand out toward the handprint, then pulled it away. "Nope," she said out loud, "I ain't touching that."

But it seemed like her hand wouldn't listen to her head, because the next thing she knew, her hand was resting there in that handprint, a perfect fit. With the other hand, Pearl traced the letters carved in the cement. R–U–B–Y. She tried to imagine herself as twelve-year-old Ruby, watching her daddy put up this clothesline. Maybe Ivy watched, too. The peach orchard was probably full of peaches back then. Maybe after twelve-year-old Ruby pushed her hand into that wet cement, she had gone out there and had herself a juicy peach.

Pearl felt the sun on the back of her neck. She lay down in the dirt and put her cheek on the warm cement, keeping her hand in the handprint. Then she went ahead and let the crying come. She cried so loud she bet that big happy family up there at Moonpie's house could probably hear her, but she didn't care.

When she was all cried out, Pearl got up and wiped her face on her sleeve. She went back to the tomato garden and picked a bright red tomato. She brought the tomato back over to the clothesline and dropped it—splat—right on Ruby's handprint.

10

"I feel terrible leaving you alone every day," Ivy said, untying her apron and reaching for the keys on a hook by the door. "You sure you don't want to come into town with me?"

Pearl shook her head while she scraped coffee-cake crumbs onto her fork with her finger.

"Maybe you and Moon can go for a bike ride," Ivy said. She stooped down and examined her reflection in the toaster, trying to tuck her frizzled hair behind her ears.

"You ought to wear makeup," Pearl said.

Ivy chuckled.

"No, I mean it," Pearl said, cutting herself another piece of coffee cake.

"You sound just like Ruby," Ivy said. "She was all the time trying to get me to use some kind of lipstick or eye shadow or something of hers." She shook her head, sending her curls back into her face.

"I got my own makeup kit," Pearl said.

"Well, I can't say that I approve of that." Ivy jiggled the keys in her hand. "You know, when we was little, me and Ruby went to a church that didn't allow girls to wear makeup."

Pearl stopped eating and looked at Ivy. "Really?"

"That's right." Ivy pointed a key at Pearl. "Your granddaddy used to have a conniption fit when Ruby came prancing in here all gussied up with lipstick and all."

"He did?"

"Hoooowheee. You never heard such carrying on in your life."

"Like what?"

"Oh, he'd be calling her the devil and all. Saying how she was the bride of Satan and we was all going to pay for her sins. He was all the time saying our house would be struck by lightning and burn to the ground, taking her and her sins with it and me and him, too."

"What'd Mama do?"

Ivy snorted and flapped her hand. "Shoot, she'd just laugh and run back there and put on more makeup. That's the way she was. Whatever you didn't want her to do, why, she'd do it ten times more and make sure you knew it."

"Did her daddy hate her?" Pearl said.

Ivy's mouth dropped open slightly. She sat across from Pearl, still clutching the keys. "No, of course not."

"Why not?"

Ivy gazed out the window. "That man never hated nobody in his life. Scared more than a few people, I reckon, but sure never hated nobody."

"She hate him?"

Ivy looked at Pearl. "Well now, I couldn't say. Sure acted like it sometimes." She pushed her hair behind her ears again and fiddled with the keys in her hand. "She ever talk about him at all?"

"Nope."

Ivy's eyes narrowed slightly. "When he died I didn't even know where she was. I called around a few places, but then I give up. I cut the obituary out of the paper and sent it to where I thought she might be, but I never heard nothing. Maybe she got it and maybe she didn't. I don't know." Ivy got up and took the coffee cake to the counter. "You know whether or not she ever got it?" she said, her back to Pearl. "Four years ago. July."

"She never said nothing about it if she did," Pearl said. She watched the back of Ivy's head. Her curls were jiggling, and Pearl figured she was either mad or crying. Seemed like the mention of Ruby usually caused one or the other with Ivy.

"Lord, look at the time," Ivy said, grabbing the keys off the table and heading out the door. "Genevieve's gonna kill me if I ain't there for the lunch shift." She pushed the screen open and looked back at Pearl. "You gonna be all right?"

Pearl nodded and Ivy disappeared, letting the screen door slam behind her.

Pearl walked up the road toward Moonpie's, thinking about Ruby and that church and her granddaddy saying those things about the devil. Just before the road curved, she heard music coming from Moonpie's house. A radio. When she got closer, she could tell it was some kind of country music. That twangy, hillbilly kind with banjos and fiddles.

When the house came into view, Pearl saw someone sitting out on the rickety porch. An old woman in a bathrobe. Pearl stopped. The old woman waved.

"Hey," the woman called out.

Pearl didn't move.

"Hey," the old woman called again.

"Is Moonpie here?" Pearl called out to her, not moving any closer.

"He is," the woman said. "I'm his Mama Nell. I know who you are."

Pearl moved slowly toward the house.

"You're Pearl," Mama Nell said. "Come here so I can see your face." She reached a shaky hand toward Pearl. Her bony arm stuck out from the sleeve of her bathrobe.

Pearl walked up to the porch and stopped, feeling suddenly shy. She looked at her feet and felt herself blush.

"Look here," Mama Nell said in a croaky voice. "Let me see your face."

Pearl looked up. Mama Nell squinted at her, then grinned a toothless grin. "You're Ruby's girl, all right." Then she laughed a cackling kind of laugh.

"You knew her?" Pearl said.

"Sure I knew her. I been here all my life. Knew her. Knew your granddaddy. Even knew your grandmama."

"You did?"

"Sure I did."

Pearl moved closer. Mama Nell sat in a dirty, upholstered chair. Stuffing poked out of holes in the arms. Banjo music twanged out of the radio beside the chair. Mama Nell leaned over and turned it down. She sat back and wheezed, holding her bathrobe closed tight at her throat like she was cold out there in the hot sun. Her hands were bruised and covered with brown spots. Her face was creased and leathery.

"I thought you was sick," Pearl said.

Mama Nell laughed. Pearl stared at her mouth, all shriveled up where teeth should be.

"I look sick?" Mama Nell said.

"Kind of."

Mama Nell laughed again, slapping her knee. Then she coughed a rattling cough and wiped her eyes with a balled-up tissue.

"If I didn't know better, I'd swear that was Ruby Patterson just said that." Mama Nell wiped at her mouth with the same balled-up tissue. "Sit down. Moonpie's fixing my lunch."

Pearl sat on the edge of the porch. Mama Nell was barefoot. Her feet were purple and swollen, her toenails thick and yellow. Pearl had never seen an old person's feet before.

Just then a dog came out from under the porch. The boniest, ugliest, mangiest dog Pearl had ever seen. It limped up onto the porch, teetering slightly with every step.

"There's my Skeeter," Mama Nell said, rubbing the dog under his chin.

The dog flopped down and put his head on Mama Nell's ugly feet. His face was gray. One eyelid drooped closed. Flies landed on him, but he didn't move a whisker.

"Is that dog old?" Pearl asked.

Mama Nell laughed that cackly laugh again. "Nope. Not Skeeter. Not me, neither." She grinned at Pearl, and Pearl felt silly, like a little kid.

Moonpie came out of the house, carrying a rusty metal tray.

"Hey," he said to Pearl. "I didn't know you was here." He put the tray in front of Mama Nell, resting it across the arms of the dirty chair.

Mama Nell inspected the tray in front of her through narrowed eyes. A steaming bowl of something, bacon on a paper plate, and a can of beer. She lifted the beer in a toast toward Pearl. "To Ruby," she said, then took a long drink, her throat bobbing up and down in her skinny neck as she swallowed.

She sniffed the bowl on the tray and smiled. "Oatmeal and brown sugar," she said. "You ever have that?"

"No, ma'am."

She poked a spoon toward Pearl. "Ought to," she said.

Moon sat on the edge of the porch beside Pearl. His tissue-paper eyelids were red and swollen. He wiped at his nose with the back of his hand.

Mama Nell made slurpy noises as she ate the oatmeal. Pearl tried not to look at those ugly feet there on the porch beside her. She didn't know how that dog could stand having his head on top of those yellow toenails.

"Here you go, Skeeter boy." Mama Nell tossed a piece of bacon onto the porch beside the dog. Pearl and Moon watched Skeeter sniff and lick the bacon, then swallow it whole in one gulp. He dropped his head back onto Mama Nell's feet, as if eating that bacon had taken every ounce of energy he had.

"One of them social workers called this morning," Moon said to Pearl.

"How come?"

"Wants to come up here and talk to Mama Nell."

"About what?"

"About me, I think."

"What about you?" Pearl asked.

"Aw, for criminy's sake," Mama Nell said in a loud, croaky voice. "Why you getting all broke up over them folks, Moon?"

Moon hung his head so low Pearl thought he was going to topple over into the yard. Tears dropped onto his freckled knees.

Mama Nell coughed another rattly cough, then took a swig of beer.

"You got to trust me on this, Moonpie," she said, putting a bony hand on Moon's back.

"What if they send me away?" Moon said in a tiny little-boy voice.

"Send you away?" Mama Nell hollered so loud even old Skeeter lifted his head. "Where you think they gonna send you?"

"Maybe to my mama."

Mama Nell grabbed Moon's shoulder and gave it a shake. "You listen to me, boy. Ain't nobody sending you nowhere. I been here for you every day of your life, ain't I?"

Moon's head was still hanging low and his shoulders were shaking. He closed his eyes. Pearl could see the little blue veins through his tissue-paper eyelids. He wiped at his nose and eyes with his T-shirt. "Yes, ma'am," he said.

"Well then, what makes you think I'm gonna let anybody send you anywhere?" Mama Nell cocked her head and waited.

" 'Cause you're so sick," Moon said. The silence that followed nearly swallowed them up. Pearl fidgeted a little, scared to look at Mama Nell. She watched the flies buzzing around Skeeter.

Mama Nell rubbed her hand around on Moon's

back and said, "I ain't never gonna be too sick to take care of my Moonpie."

Moon lifted his head and looked up at Mama Nell with a look of pure love. He put his head on her knee and let her stroke his cantaloupe hair with her brown-spotted hand. Pearl watched the two of them, her head all whirling around with mixed-up thoughts. Like how come Moonpie got to have so many people loving him? What could she do to make somebody love her? And if she wanted to love somebody back, who should it be? Mama? Was she supposed to love a person just because that person happened to be her mama? Did a person just get handed love, like a prize on a silver tray, or did a person have to earn it?

Then, right in the middle of all those whirling thoughts, Mama Nell said, "Somebody go get me another beer."

That night Pearl sat with her back propped against the pillows and looked down at the postcard in her lap. Fort Sumter. Charleston, South Carolina. She had taken this one to school last year when her class was studying the Civil War. She had stood in front of the room and showed the postcard and told the class that she had been to Fort Sumter. But she hadn't. Never even been close.

She had thought maybe those kids would think that

was nice, going to Fort Sumter and all. And maybe they would think she was nice, too. Maybe one of them would call her up sometime and invite her over. But nobody ever did.

Pearl chewed on the end of her pen, thinking. Then she wrote:

> *Dear Mama,*
>
> *Moonpie is worried about social workers sending him away and Mama Nell is supposed to be sick but she looks okay to me except for her feet. I was thinking maybe I should get me a dog so I could have something deserving of my love. What do you think?*
>
> *Love,*
Pearl

11

"Ruby killed a chicken one time," Ivy said. "Threw a brick just as hard as she could."

Pearl and Ivy sat on the porch steps watching the chickens strut around the yard.

"How come?" Pearl said.

Ivy shrugged. "Just felt like it, I guess." She scraped at a spot of dried-up food on the uniform she wore to work. "Daddy smacked her legs with a flyswatter and she didn't even cry."

Ivy held her hand over her eyes and squinted up the road. "There he is." She stood up and smoothed the back of her skirt. "Now remember," she said, "I'll be a tad late. John Dee and I are going to run them errands for Mama Nell. You be sure and tell Moonpie we're getting them prescriptions filled, okay?"

"Okay."

Pearl watched John Dee's van bouncing down the road toward them. He honked the horn and waved as he pulled into the gravel driveway.

Ivy grinned and waved back. "Don't forget about that fried chicken in the refrigerator," she said, pushing Pearl's hair out of her eyes. "There's coleslaw in there, too, okay?"

"Okay."

"See you later, then." Ivy started down the steps, then turned back and put her warm hands on Pearl's cheeks. She didn't say anything. Just smiled.

Pearl felt good and smiled back. She loved that about Ivy, how she didn't have to talk to let you know something.

"Okay, I *really* got to go," Ivy said, hurrying out to the driveway.

When Ivy opened the door of the van, John Dee leaned over and called out, "Hey, Pearl."

Pearl flapped her hand in his direction. She watched the rusty van drive away, Ivy's voice drifting out the window.

Pearl spit her chewing gum out into the dusty yard and watched the chickens scramble over to peck at it. She tried to imagine herself killing a chicken. She picked up an invisible brick and heaved it, sending chickens squawking and flapping in every direction.

"What you doing?" Moon called from the road.

Pearl jumped. Dern, why does he have to be so sneaky, she thought.

Moon dropped his bike on the side of the road and joined Pearl in the yard.

"What do you want to do?" he said.

"Let's go back to that graveyard."

Moon shook his head and said, "Naw."

"Why not?"

"Just don't want to."

"Let's go talk to Mama Nell," Pearl said.

"About what?"

"I don't know. Just stuff."

Moon shook his head again. "She's sleeping."

"Then I'm going in and watch TV." Pearl turned and started up the front steps.

"I know where there's buried treasure," Moon said.

Pearl stopped. She narrowed her eyes and studied Moonpie. "Where?"

Moon hung his head. "Never mind," he said.

"Never mind!" Pearl threw her hands up. "What do you mean 'Never mind'? What are you? Just a big liar or something?"

Moon frowned at Pearl. "I ain't a liar."

"Then where's this so-called buried treasure?"

"It's a secret," Moon said.

"Then why'd you tell me about it?" Pearl watched Moon shuffling around in the dirt like a nervous hen. "You ain't supposed to tell somebody you know a secret if you ain't gonna *tell* the secret." Pearl put her hands on her hips. Didn't he know the rules of life?

Moon turned and headed toward the road. When he reached for his bike, Pearl raced after him. "Wait," she said. "I didn't mean that. I know you ain't lying. I believe you. Show me the treasure. I won't tell nobody."

Moon eyed her through his greasy hair. "You swear?"

Pearl crossed her heart with her finger and held her palm up. "I swear."

Moon dropped his bike. "Okay."

Pearl followed him to the shed in the backyard.

"It's in there." Moon pointed.

"Well, show me," Pearl snapped.

Moon's eyes darted around the yard. He turned and looked behind him, toward the house, then up the road. Just when Pearl was beginning to think she was going to have to give him a shove or something, he pushed the creaky shed door open and stepped inside. Pearl went in after him, squinting into the darkness. He pushed aside damp, dusty cardboard boxes, rusty garden tools, and paint cans, then stooped to brush dirt off a board half-buried in the dirt floor. When he lifted the board, Pearl craned her neck to see.

"What's under there?" she whispered, peering over Moonpie's shoulder at the hole in the floor.

Moon grunted as he pulled up a metal tackle box. He brushed the dirt off and opened it.

"It's too dark in here," Pearl said. "Bring it outside."

"No way," Moon said. "Just look quick and then I'm putting it back." He reached into the tackle box and pulled out a mildewed canvas bag. "Here, look quick."

Pearl opened the bag and peered inside. "Wow."

She reached into the bag and scooped up a handful of coins.

"Silver dollars," Moon said.

"How many?"

"Ninety-seven."

"Shoot, that ain't so much," Pearl said. "You think that's treasure?"

"They're real old. Ivy said nearly every one of them is most likely worth a lot more than a dollar."

"Really?"

Moon nodded. "Let's put 'em back," he said, reaching for the bag.

Pearl yanked it away, holding it against her side with both arms. "Wait a minute. You got to tell me more than that."

"Like what?"

"Like where'd these come from and why are they here."

Moon licked his finger and wiped dirt off his knees.

"Well?" Pearl watched him, sitting there on the damp dirt floor, his eyes looking everywhere but at her. "Well?" Pearl yelled.

"They was your granddaddy's," Moon said.

"How do you know?"

"He showed 'em to me."

Pearl stared at Moonpie. "*Showed* 'em to you?"

Moon nodded.

Pearl sat down, resting the bag of coins in her lap. Now, *this* was a revelation. It had never occurred to her that Moonpie had ever met her granddaddy. "You met my granddaddy?" she said.

Moon nodded again.

"When?"

"I was real little."

"How little?"

"I don't know. Six or seven, maybe. I don't hardly remember."

"What'd he look like?"

Moon looked up at the ceiling. "Well, I don't remember much. Had a big ole beard. I remember that."

"What else?"

87

"I don't know."

Pearl grabbed Moon's arm and squeezed. "You got to remember," she said. "I need to know."

"He had rotten teeth," Moon said.

Pearl pushed Moon's arm away from her and sat back against the side of the shed. A big ole beard and rotten teeth. Besides Ivy, this was her only link to family and all Moon remembered was a big ole beard and rotten teeth.

"I think he was nice," Moon said real soft.

Pearl looked at him. "Really?" she said.

Moon nodded. "He showed me this treasure, didn't he?"

"What's it doing out here?"

" 'Cause of fire."

"Fire?"

"Yeah." Moon looked at the bag of coins in Pearl's lap, then leaned forward to look out the shed door. "Ivy said he was afraid his house was going to burn down. He always said never keep your treasures in the house in case of fire."

Pearl snapped her fingers. "The bride of Satan," she said. "The makeup and all. That's how come he thought the house was going to burn. 'Cause of Mama's makeup. 'Cause of the lightning."

Moon squeezed his eyebrows together and looked at Pearl.

"Oh, never mind," she said. "Here, put this back." She dropped the bag of coins in Moonpie's lap.

"Does Ivy know this is here?" she asked.

"Sure she does," Moon said. "She comes out here every once in a while to make sure it's still here." Moon looked toward the door again. "You can't tell nobody I showed you, okay? I'm the only one besides Ivy knows this is here."

"Okay."

Pearl watched Moon put the bag back in the tackle box, the tackle box in the hole, and the board over the hole.

Imagine that. Her very own granddaddy, big ole beard, rotten teeth, and all, sitting in this very same shed showing little Moonpie that bag of silver dollars. What had she been doing at that very moment, she wondered. Maybe riding on a Greyhound bus. Maybe waking up on a dirty couch in a room full of strangers. Maybe watching Ruby dance on the hood of a car.

It was hard to say. Could have been any of those things.

12

Pearl smelled bacon. She stared up at that crack that looked like mountains on the ceiling, then sat up and looked at herself in the dusty mirror over the dresser. Her hair was stringy and tangled, her bangs hanging in clumps over her eyes. Her face was sunburned and her eyes kind of puffy. She hated the way she looked.

"You are one beautiful girl," Ruby always said. "Just like me," she'd add. "You and me, Pearl and Ruby, two gems of the world."

When the phone rang, Pearl saw her face tighten up. Felt that familiar knot in her stomach. She hated herself for having that feeling every time the phone rang, every time a car came down the road or the front door opened.

She smoothed her hair with her hand and went down the hall to the kitchen. Ivy was hanging up the phone.

"There you are," she said. "I was wondering when you were going to get up."

Pearl yawned and sat at the table.

"Fried or scrambled?" Ivy said.

"Scrambled."

"I sure am glad to have a day off, I can tell you that." Ivy cracked two eggs into a bowl and beat them with a fork. "John Dee's coming over to fix that dern washing machine." The frying pan sizzled when she poured the eggs in. "What you doing today?"

Pearl shrugged.

"Maybe we should go shopping," Ivy said. "Them sneakers of yours are ready for the trash heap."

"I ain't got any money," Pearl said, watching Ivy scrape the eggs onto a plate.

Ivy chuckled. "I got money."

"Seems like if Mama was gonna dump me off on you she would've thought about leaving some money." Pearl twirled the salt shaker around. It tipped over, sending a trail of salt across the table. "But I reckon she needed to save her money for herself. You know, in case she wanted a new dress or some jewelry or something. Or nail polish. You know how much she likes nail polish. I bet she even liked nail polish when she was little, didn't she?" Pearl wiped at her eyes and chewed the inside of her cheek, trying like everything to keep from crying. "Besides," she added, "why would she want to go and give up her money for me?"

Pearl squeezed her fingernails into the palms of her hands. Why had she gone and started talking like this, she wondered. She hadn't meant to. All she'd meant to do was eat scrambled eggs.

Ivy set a plate of steaming eggs in front of Pearl and sat down. Pearl picked up the fork, but couldn't seem to make herself start eating.

Ivy leaned toward Pearl. "This ain't your fault, Pearl," she said.

"Mamas don't leave their kid behind unless that kid ain't worth keeping," Pearl said.

"Who told you that?"

"No one."

"Then how do you know that?"

Pearl threw her fork onto the table with a clang. "Any idiot knows that." She dropped both hands in her lap and slumped back in her seat. "She tells me lies all the time."

"What kind of lies?"

"Like me and her are two gems of the world. I ain't no gem and she don't think so neither or she wouldn't've left me." Pearl saw tears drop onto her lap before she realized she was crying. She felt Ivy's hand rubbing her back.

"I think Ruby's just confused," Ivy said.

"Confused about what?"

"Well, I ain't sure exactly. Just confused."

Pearl pushed a piece of limp bacon from one side of her plate to the other. "Well, I'm confused, too," she said.

"I'm sure you are, my little Pearl," Ivy said. "I'm sure you are."

One of the cats rubbed against Pearl's legs and she pushed it away. "Maybe I could work at the diner," she said.

"Work at the diner?" Ivy sat back down across from Pearl.

"So I could earn some money. Then I can pay you."

"Pay me for what?"

"For living here. You know, for my food and all. And for sneakers. Stuff like that."

Ivy reached across the table and took both of Pearl's hands in hers. "Sugar, you can't live with me forever."

Well, stab my heart, Pearl thought when she heard those words. Just stab my heart right through. She jerked her hands away and looked at Ivy to make sure she wasn't joking. The serious look on Ivy's face told Pearl she wasn't. "Then where am I going to live?" she said. Her voice came out all trembly.

93

"With Ruby, honey. She's your mama. We've got to find her and make her come back."

"How are we going to do that?"

"Well, I'm hoping the police will find her," Ivy said.

"What do you mean?"

"I mean, 'cause the police might be looking for her."

"Why might the police be looking for her?" Pearl felt scared. Maybe Ruby had gone and robbed a bank or something.

" 'Cause I filed a report," Ivy said. "You know, a missing-person report. That's what you have to do when a person is missing. So they can find 'em. The police, that is. So the police can find the missing person." Ivy's neck was getting those red splotches. She scratched it, leaving white fingernail marks.

"When did you do that?" Pearl asked.

"Do what?"

"File a report," Pearl snapped.

"A while back." Ivy pushed the plate toward Pearl. "Your eggs are getting cold."

"Why didn't you tell me you did that?"

"Well, I don't know. I just, you know . . . I guess I should have, but I . . . Pearl, honey, school's gonna be starting soon. We got to figure out what to do."

"So what happens?" Pearl said. "The police tell her to get on back and get her daughter or else she'll go to jail? So she comes running back here 'cause she don't want to go to jail? They probably ain't got very good nail polish in jail."

Pearl could see Ivy's mouth twitching and she just dared her to laugh, but she didn't.

"I'm sorry, Pearl," Ivy said. "I should've told you. I was wrong not to tell you."

Pearl stood up so fast she knocked the chair over with a crash that sent the cat scurrying out of the kitchen. "Besides," she said, "you filed the wrong kind of report. You should've filed a crazy-person report. Them police ain't looking for a missing person, they're looking for a crazy person." Pearl paced around the kitchen table. Ivy watched her, clutching her hands together so hard her knuckles turned white.

"She ain't a gem of the world," Pearl went on. "She's a crazy person."

Ivy nodded. "You might be right."

"She tried to make me steal a ham one time. 'Put that ham in your backpack, Pearlie May,' she said. 'No, I won't,' I said. She kept on and on and I kept saying no and then I laid on the floor and cried. I still remember that cold floor with sticky stuff on it. So she walked right out of that store and got in the car and I ran out after her and she locked the door and wouldn't let me in. I beat on the window and she rolled it down just a tiny little crack and said, 'Go away, little girl. You ain't mine.' And I said, 'Yes I am,'

95

and she said, 'I can't see you. You're invisible,' and I been invisible ever since." Pearl sank into a chair and put her head on the table and cried.

Ivy didn't say anything for a while. Just smoothed Pearl's hair over and over. Then she said, "You ain't invisible to me, Pearl. I can see you just fine—and you look like an angel to me."

Pearl lifted her head and looked at her reflection in the toaster. She might be invisible to her mama, but there she was in the toaster, real as anything. An angel? Not hardly. She still had the same ratty hair, same sunburned face. Why couldn't she change, she wondered. Turn into somebody else. Somebody who really was a gem of the world.

That night she took out the shoebox and dumped her postcards onto the bed. She searched through the pile, finally finding the one she wanted. A kudzu-covered barn in Travelers Rest, South Carolina.

Dear Mama,
Ivy asked me to stay here and
be her daughter and I said yes.
Goodbye.

Love,
Pearl

13

Pearl sat on the back porch steps and looked out at the old peach orchard. It had been nearly four weeks since Ruby had gone off the deep end. Pearl was still trying to stop her feelings from getting yanked around.

Mama, come back.

Mama, don't come back.

Mama, come back.

Mama, don't come back.

How could a person want something and not want something at the very same time?

July had turned into August, but the air was still thick and damp with heat. Pearl held her hair off her forehead and flapped her hand in front of her face, trying to stir up a breeze.

She should have gone to the diner with Moonpie and Ivy. At least there was air-conditioning. She walked out to the garden. Tomato plants sprawled in tangled clumps on the ground. A green tomato had been half eaten by a rabbit. Pearl tossed it into the bushes. She looked up toward Moonpie's house.

Pearl had a thought in her head that wouldn't go away. The thought had been whirling around all night and all day and driving Pearl crazy. The thought was about Mama Nell. About how Mama Nell knew her mama back a long time ago and Mama Nell was liable to up and die any minute now. Pearl figured if she didn't get herself on up there and talk to Mama Nell, she might find herself wishing she had. She picked a ripe tomato and headed up the hill.

When she caught sight of Moonpie's house, Pearl stopped and listened. Silence. When she got to the porch, she stopped again. Skeeter was lying by the screen door. He lifted his head and looked at Pearl, then let his head fall back to the floor with a groan.

"Mama Nell?" Pearl called out.

Nothing.

Pearl climbed the porch steps and knocked on the rickety screen door.

"Mama Nell? It's me, Pearl."

Still nothing.

Okay, Pearl thought, if Mama Nell's dead, I'm getting out of here.

She knocked again.

Mama Nell's gravelly voice came through the screen.

"Who's that?"

"It's me, Pearl."

"What for?"

"Uh, I . . . well, I . . ." Pearl looked down at the tomato in her hand. "I brought you a tomato."

"Gives me heartburn," Mama Nell said. "It ain't a beefsteak anyways, is it?"

"No, it's a tomato."

Mama Nell cackled. "You don't know much about nothing, do you?"

Pearl squinted through the screen door. "Can I come in?"

"What for?"

" 'Cause I want to," Pearl said.

Mama Nell cackled again, then coughed a rattly cough.

Pearl opened the door and stepped inside. She wrinkled her nose at the smell. Cabbage or something.

Mama Nell sat in her ratty old chair with a cat in her lap. Wads of tissue littered the floor at her feet. Those swollen, purple feet. She wore a thin, dirty nightgown over an undershirt, the kind of undershirt that old men wear.

"Moonpie might like this tomato," Pearl said. She felt silly. Maybe coming up here wasn't such a good idea after all.

"He might." Mama Nell held out a shaky hand. Pearl gave her the tomato. Then she decided not to beat around the bush.

"What was my mama like when she was a little girl?" she said.

Mama Nell's eyes wrinkled up in a smile but her mouth stayed set—turned down and grumpy-looking.

"Who's your mama?" Mama Nell said.

Pearl's stomach squeezed up tight. Maybe Mama Nell had gone senile. Maybe she didn't remember much.

"Ruby," Pearl said. "Ruby Patterson."

Mama Nell chuckled, causing the cat on her lap to look up with an irritated look. "Just testing you," she said.

Shoot, thought Pearl. This old woman's crazy. Pearl figured she might as well leave, but she didn't. She sat on the edge of the bed and waited.

"Ruby Patterson was full of the devil, I can tell you that," Mama Nell said.

"What besides that?" Pearl said.

"Used to smoke cigarettes with Moon's mama under

that porch out there." Mama Nell nodded toward the front porch. "Went around soreheaded all the time, just daring somebody to knock the chip off her shoulder."

"What else?"

Mama Nell coughed so long and hard that Pearl stood up, wondering if she should do something. The cat jumped down and scurried into the kitchen.

When Mama Nell finally stopped coughing, she wiped her mouth with a tissue and tossed it onto the floor. "That little thing didn't want nothing in this world 'cept for her daddy to notice her like he did Ivy," she said.

Pearl sat back down on the bed. Well now, she thought, here was something to chew on.

"Just went about it all wrong was the problem," Mama Nell said. She wiped her eyes with the hem of her nightgown. Pearl looked away quickly. She sure didn't want to see what was up under there.

"How'd she do that?" Pearl asked. "Go about it the wrong way, I mean?"

"Caused trouble every dern minute of the day, that's how. Made her daddy notice her, all right." Mama Nell shook her head and stared out the front door. "Law, you could hear that man hollerin'."

"Really?"

Mama Nell chuckled. "Course, you could hear Ruby

hollerin' right back. She liked to drove that old coot crazy the way she stood up to him. Not like Ivy, I can tell you that. Ivy, she always done things right by the book, that girl did."

A fly buzzed around Mama Nell's face. Pearl watched it land on a tuft of the old woman's thin white hair.

"Ole Ruby Patterson," Mama Nell went on, "stirring things up like a tornado."

"What'd she look like?"

"Look like?"

Pearl nodded.

"Looked like you," Mama Nell said. "Spittin' image."

"You ever see her cry?"

Mama Nell squinted at Pearl. "Cry?"

Pearl felt like saying, "Is there an echo in here?" the way her mama would have, but she kept quiet.

"Yeah, I seen her cry," Mama Nell said. "That make you happy? Her crying?"

Pearl looked down at the floor.

"What you looking all hangdog for?" Mama Nell said. "Nothing wrong with being happy."

"I ain't happy," Pearl said.

"You sure ain't. You're as soreheaded as that Ruby."

Pearl stared at Mama Nell. Why was this old woman getting on her case like this?

"I ain't soreheaded," Pearl said.

"Ain't you?"

"No." Pearl held her chin up and looked that old woman square in the eye. "Besides, if I was, I'd have a right to be."

"Ha!" Mama Nell flapped a bony, bruised-up hand at Pearl.

Pearl felt her face heat up with anger. "Just 'cause I look like her on the outside don't mean I'm like her on the inside," she said so loud Skeeter lifted his head again out on the porch.

Mama Nell laughed her rattly laugh.

Pearl stomped toward the door.

"She stole from me one time," Mama Nell said. "You wanna get your name in my Grudge Book, you steal from me."

Pearl stopped. She turned around and looked at Mama Nell. "What'd she steal?"

"My yellow-bird music box."

Pearl walked back to the bed and sat down.

"She was all the time admiring that thing," Mama Nell said. "Winding it up and listening to it and then winding it up again. She took it one day. Just up and took it."

"How do you know it was her that took it?" Pearl wondered why she bothered to ask that. Of course it was Ruby that took it. That was just like her.

"She had a rinky-dink little ole fort down in the orchard. I could hear that music box clear as a bell from up here." Mama Nell leaned forward and said real low, " 'Scuse me for saying so, but she wasn't exactly the sharpest tool in the shed."

Pearl frowned. "What'd you do?"

"Told her to keep her skinny butt off my property, that's what."

"Did she?"

"Sure did." Mama Nell pulled another tissue out of the box on the arm of her chair and wiped her mouth. "But ole Ruby Patterson, she didn't want nobody thinking they knew her. If she had a notion that you thought she was gonna get up on the right side of the bed, she'd get up on the left side or die trying. That's the way she was. Five years that music box was gone and then one day there it was right up on that shelf again and I ain't seen Ruby Patterson since."

Pearl followed Mama Nell's gaze to the shelf on the wall behind the bed. It was cluttered with magazines, empty soda cans, a Bible, a flashlight, a dusty statue of praying hands—and a little yellow bird on a nest of flowers.

Pearl had to use every ounce of strength she had to keep from jumping up and snatching that bird. She put her hands under her knees and looked out the door at Skeeter twitching in his sleep.

It was so quiet in the room that Pearl could hear Mama Nell's raspy breathing. She felt her chin quivering when she said, "I reckon she wasn't all bad, then."

"Bad? Who said she was bad?"

"You did."

"You hear what you wanna hear, girlie."

Pearl chewed on her lower lip and stared at that little yellow bird on the shelf. She felt Mama Nell's hand on her knee.

"Wasn't nothing wrong with Ruby that a little of her daddy's love wouldn't've cured," Mama Nell said. "But something tells me she's a hard person to love."

Pearl looked at the dirty linoleum floor. She wished Mama Nell would take that scrawny hand off her knee. Wished she wasn't sitting here in this dark, smelly old house with a sick, mean old lady. But most of all, she wished her mama wasn't a hard person to love.

14

Pearl was watering the marigolds when she saw the flashing red lights. She didn't move. Just stood there letting the water turn the red dirt into a muddy puddle. She knew right off the bat where those flashing red lights were headed, but she stood there watching anyway, like she needed to know for sure.

When the red lights turned onto the road to Moonpie's house, Pearl's brain got the message. An ambulance. Going to Moonpie's house. She threw the watering can clear across the yard and took off running, jumping over brier bushes and scrambling up the hill.

By the time Pearl got to Moon's house, the ambulance was parked out front. The flashing red lights looked creepy, going round and round, sending rays of red light through the trees and across the front of the house. Pearl stopped at the edge of the porch. Voices drifted out of the screen door.

Mama Nell's ratty old chair was out on the porch. Pearl went up and sat in it. It smelled like medicine and stale beer. She listened to the sounds coming from inside the house. Moon's voice. A man's voice. Static from a radio. Pearl could hear Skeeter under the porch whining. The sound of gravel crunching under tires made Pearl look up. John Dee's van pulled into the dirt yard and stopped.

Moonpie must have heard the van, too, because the screen door burst open and he ran out. By the time he jumped off the porch, John Dee was out of the van. The two of them headed straight for each other, arms out. When they met, they folded their arms around one another. Pearl watched, fascinated. How did they know to do that? What was it that made them both do exactly the same thing? It was almost as if they'd rehearsed the moment, like a play. Pearl was sure that she wouldn't have known what to do. She probably would have done the wrong thing. But John Dee and Moonpie did it just right, standing there in the yard holding each other like that.

The scene was interrupted when the screen door

opened and two men carried Mama Nell out on a stretcher. Pearl covered her face with her hands. She heard the ambulance door open and looked up just in time to see Mama Nell's ugly purple feet disappear inside the ambulance. The men said something to John Dee, then the ambulance bounced down the bumpy, rutted road, sending red light through the trees until it disappeared from sight.

Moonpie stood in the yard, looking so pitiful Pearl covered her face with her hands again. Then he started crying. Loud and mournful. Pearl had never heard a boy cry like that. She didn't know what to do.

John Dee knew just what to do. He put his arm around Moon and led him over to the porch. He gently pushed Moon's shoulders, making him sit on the steps, then sat beside him. Pearl watched the back of them. Moon's shoulders shaking as he cried. John Dee's big, hairy hand rubbing Moon's back. When John Dee finally spoke, Pearl jumped.

"Ivy's gonna meet us at the hospital," he said.

Moon kept on crying.

"Okay?" John Dee said, leaning over and looking up into Moon's face.

Moon's crying got softer and he looked up. His face was streaked with dirt, his eyes red and swollen. "Okay," he said in a tiny, pitiful voice.

"Why don't you go on down to the house, Pearl," John Dee said. "Ain't no need for you to go to the hospital, okay?"

Pearl wanted to argue with him, but she knew he was right. Knew she didn't belong with them. Moonpie, Ivy, John Dee, Mama Nell. They all fit together like a jigsaw puzzle. But she was the extra piece. The one that just didn't fit with the others no matter which way you turned it. No matter how hard you pushed it.

She nodded. "Okay."

"You want me to call Genevieve to come over and stay with you?" John Dee said.

Pearl shook her head.

"You want a ride down the hill?"

Pearl shook her head again.

"Well . . ." John Dee stood up and nudged Moonpie. "We better go, then."

Pearl watched the two of them climb into the van.

"We'll call you, okay?" John Dee hollered out the window as they headed down the hill.

Pearl lay on the couch and stared at the television. She had turned the sound off. She watched the silent screen. A cartoon bear held a stick of dynamite. Pearl watched the silent explosion. When the dust settled, the bear blinked out at her, his fur sticking up in black, smoking clumps.

When the phone rang, Pearl raced to the kitchen. Her heart beat so fast she clutched both hands to her chest and closed her eyes for a moment before picking up the receiver.

"Hello?"

"Pearl?" Ivy's voice sounded all shaky. "This is Ivy."

"Hey."

"Mama Nell's passed on," Ivy said.

Pearl waited.

"Pearl?"

"Yeah."

"You okay?"

"Yeah."

"Well, uh, I don't . . . I guess . . ." Ivy's voice cracked. Pearl waited. "We'll be home before dark, okay?"

"Okay."

"You heat up them pork chops from last night, okay?"

"Okay."

Pearl could hear Ivy's breathing. "Ivy?"

"What?"

"You all right?"

There was a brief moment of silence, then Ivy said, "Yes, sweetheart, I'm all right."

"That's good," Pearl said. "That you're all right, I mean."

Silence.

"Ivy?"

"Hmmm?"

"Never mind."

"I got to go now, okay?"

"Okay. Bye."

Click.

Pearl went out the back door and straight up to Moon's house. Skeeter was lying out in the dirt yard. His tail thumped a couple of slow thumps on the ground. Pearl stooped to pet him, rubbing her hand down his sides. His ribs showed through his dirty fur. She ran her hand over them. Bump, bump, bump. She put her arms around him, resting her head on his bony side. She could hear his heart beating slow and steady beneath his mangy fur.

Then she went up on the porch and peered through the screen door. It was dark and spooky-looking inside. Pearl went in. She hurried to the shelf over the bed, took that yellow-bird music box, and ran down the hill to Ivy's. She went straight back to her room and put the bird inside her shoebox. She snatched a postcard from the box, then sat on the bed and wrote:

But she didn't know what to say. She stared at the postcard, chewing on the end of her pen. Then she tore the card into tiny pieces and threw them in the shoebox with the yellow bird.

15

Hardly anybody came to the funeral. A few old people from town. Genevieve and Jay from the diner. Ivy called down to Macon to try and find Moonpie's mama, but the phone number she had was no good.

"I can't hardly even believe that," Ivy had said to Pearl real low so Moonpie wouldn't hear. "The woman just up and moves and don't tell nobody nothing."

Moon's brother in Lavonia said he was coming, but he didn't show up.

"Wouldn't you think the man would wonder what in this world was going to happen to Moonpie?" Ivy had said.

Pearl had just nodded.

"Well, obviously he don't give a dern," Ivy said under her breath. "Didn't even mention the poor child's name."

Pearl had never been to a funeral before. She sat with Moonpie and Ivy and John Dee. Moon cried so much his face was red and he hiccuped through the whole service. Ivy kept her arm around him, telling him how Mama Nell had been an angel on this earth and now she was watching over them from heaven. Pearl looked up at the ceiling. She tried to imagine that grumpy old lady flapping around up in the sky with angel wings and swollen purple feet.

After the service, Genevieve came by Ivy's house and everyone sat on the porch not saying much. Ivy kept trying to get people to eat, but it seemed like John Dee was the only one who had any appetite.

When Genevieve left, Pearl sat on the steps next to Moonpie.

"Hey," she said.

"Hey."

"Genevieve brought some of them little hot dogs. You want some?"

"Naw."

"You want me to go get Skeeter?" Pearl said.

"Naw," Moon said. "I reckon he likes it better up there." They had tried to get Skeeter to stay down at Ivy's with Moon, but he kept going back up to the house. Pearl had gone to get him a couple of times and had found him lying on the porch by Mama Nell's chair, looking about as pitiful as a dog can look.

"What about your cat?" Pearl said. "You want me to feed it?"

Moon shook his head, then wiped his runny nose with the back of his hand.

Pearl looked out at the yard. The few patches of grass were dried up and yellow. A thin layer of red dust coated the walkway.

"Sure is dry, ain't it?" Pearl said.

"Yeah."

"Moon?"

"Hmmm."

"I'm sorry about Mama Nell."

Moon's face crumpled up and the tears rolled down his freckled cheeks.

Pearl looked away.

"What's going to happen to me now?" Moon said real soft and pitiful.

Pearl looked at him. Then she did something that surprised them both. She put her arm around him.

"Beats me," she said. "But I know how you feel."

It was over a week before Pearl could get Moonpie to do anything besides sit on the porch. He had been sleeping on the couch at night, hugging his grimy pillow and not even taking his clothes off. He'd get up in the morning, smooth his hair down with his hand, and sit on the porch for most of the day. Pearl had come up with about a million ideas to pass the time—picking tomatoes, walking Skeeter, building a fort—but Moon wasn't interested in anything but sitting. Finally one day Pearl said, "Let's ride bikes into town," and he said, "Okay."

She rode ahead of him, struggling to keep Ivy's beat-up old bike from wobbling into the ditch that ran along the road. Every now and then, she looked over her shoulder to make sure Moon was still there.

When they got to town, they leaned their bikes against the side of the diner and went in. It smelled like grease and onions. Genevieve looked up from wiping the counter.

"Well, look what the cat drug in," she said. "What y'all doing?"

"Nothing," Pearl said.

"You looking for Ivy?"

"Naw. Just looking for something to do."

"She ain't here anyways."

"Where is she?"

"Her and John Dee went somewhere, I think." The bell on the diner door tinkled, and two men in overalls came in. "I got to wait on these folks. You all get your-self a corn muffin," Genevieve said.

Pearl lifted the glass dome and took two muffins. She handed one to Moonpie.

"Let's go," she said.

Outside, the sun was so bright Pearl could see the blue veins through Moon's pale skin. He looked a lot younger than eleven, standing there with white, scabby knees, eating that corn muffin. Pearl had an urge to hold his hand, like he was a little kid, but she didn't.

"Let's just walk around, okay?" Pearl said.

Moon nodded.

They walked for nearly an hour, stopping from time to time to peer into a store window. Then they bought sodas and sat on a bench. Across the street was a brick building with a peeling, weathered sign. Darwood Town Offices.

Moon tossed his empty can into a wastebasket. "There's Ivy and John Dee," he said, pointing.

"Where?"

"Over there."

Pearl looked in the direction he pointed. Ivy and John Dee were coming out of the building across the street. They were holding hands. Ivy was laughing. They walked fast, almost skipping. When they got to Ivy's car, they stopped and hugged. Then they kissed. Right there in front of anybody who wanted to watch.

"What do you think they're doing?" Pearl said, shielding her eyes from the sun.

Moon shrugged. "I don't know."

"Why would they be in them offices, I wonder."

Moon shrugged again.

Pearl could feel herself getting irritated.

"Well, what do you *think* they were doing in there?" she said.

Moon turned toward her in that slow way of his and blinked a long blink. "I don't know," he said.

By the time Pearl turned to look again, Ivy's car was disappearing around the corner, puffs of black smoke trailing behind it.

Pearl had a bad feeling in her stomach. Something was going on. She just knew it. Something that was liable to stir things up for her again. Life had begun to settle down a little bit. It was time for an upset. That's the way things went for Pearl. She had a feel for upset—like radar—and she felt it coming.

16

Pearl's radar had been right. The upset came that very day.

By the time she and Moon got home, Ivy and John Dee were there, sitting in lawn chairs in the backyard. Ivy was shelling black-eyed peas into a bowl on her lap. John Dee was drinking a beer and eating a tomato sandwich.

"Hey, you two," Ivy called out when Pearl and Moonpie came around the corner of the house, pushing their bikes. "Where you been?"

"In town," Pearl said. She pushed the bike into the shed and sat on the ground near Ivy. "What're y'all doing?"

Ivy looked at John Dee and smiled. "Nothing really. Just sitting here wishing for some rain on that garden out yonder." She turned to Moonpie. "How are you doing, sweetheart?"

Moon reached for some peas, then sat on the ground next to Ivy and began shelling. "Fine," he said, tossing peas into the bowl. He looked up at Ivy. "Maybe I'll go up to the house and check on things," he said. "You know, Skeeter and all."

Ivy put the bowl on the ground and stood up. "I'll go, too," she said. "I bet them sunflowers are needing some water."

But Moon didn't move. He just sat there, staring at the peas in his hand. Finally he said, "Ivy?"

Ivy raised her eyebrows and waited.

"What's going to happen to me?" he said. "Where am I going to go? Who'll I live with?"

Pearl sat up straighter and watched Ivy's face.

Ivy sat back down in the lawn chair. She looked at John Dee, then cupped her hands around Moonpie's face. "Me and John Dee got some news for you, sweetheart," she said. "I was waiting to make sure everything was going to work out before I told you, but things are looking pretty good now—so here goes."

She sat back and took a breath. "Me and John Dee are getting married."

Pearl's heart flopped all the way down to her stomach. Ka-thunk. She stared at Ivy, who sat there grinning. Before that news could sink in, more news came spilling out.

"And I been talking with the social services people," Ivy said. "You know, them folks that kept calling you and all? And it looks like you're going to get to stay with me. Well, me and John Dee. Like a foster home. We filled out all them papers to be foster parents." She reached over and patted John Dee on the knee. "And soon as they make sure ole John Dee here ain't a criminal or something—and me, too, of course—it looks like everything's going to work out. For you, I mean . . . to live with me and John Dee . . . after we get married."

Pearl felt like somebody had up and punched her in the stomach. Oomph.

She hardly heard what anybody said after that. Just bits and pieces coming at her like in a dream.

". . . so happy . . ."

". . . always wanted . . ."

". . . like my own son . . ."

Pearl lay back on the ground and looked up at the sky. Maybe she really was invisible, just like Ruby had said.

During dinner, Ivy jabbered on and on about the wedding. How it was going to be a tiny little affair over at the town hall. How they were going to close the diner and have a party. How Pearl could be her maid of honor and wear a new dress and panty hose and lipstick. "And mascara," Ivy said. "You can wear some of that mascara you got in that makeup bag of yours."

John Dee kept ruffling Moonpie's hair and winking and grinning. Pearl thought he was acting silly. Moonpie seemed just pleased as punch to be the center of attention, like he was a little prince or something.

Pearl pushed her fork around her plate, sending black-eyed peas spilling over the edge and onto the table.

"Ain't you hungry, Pearl?" Ivy said.

"Not much."

"I got lemon meringue pie."

Pearl shrugged.

"How about another biscuit?" Ivy pushed the plate of biscuits across the table.

Pearl shook her head and pushed her peas around some more.

"I will," Moonpie said, reaching in front of Pearl to grab a biscuit.

Pearl glared at his skinny white arm. She ought to jab him with a fork like that man Dwayne used to do to her when she reached across the dinner table.

"Ma-maaaa, Dwayne poked me," she used to complain to Ruby. But Ruby would just say, "Hush up your whinin'."

And then one day Pearl had jabbed Dwayne back and Ruby had smacked her—whack—right upside the head and made her leave the table and not show her ugly face for the rest of the day.

"Don't show your ugly face for the rest of the day," Ruby had hollered.

Pearl had grabbed those words "ugly face" in her mind and held on tight, letting them eat away at her stomach. She had lain on the cot in the back of the house, clutching her stomach. Then she had hollered, "You said I was a gem of the world," and Ruby had hollered back, "Well, you ain't no more."

But Pearl didn't jab Moonpie.

After dinner Ivy, John Dee, and Moonpie watched TV and ate lemon meringue pie. Pearl sat on the couch with her arms folded and stared out the front door. Then she stood up and said, "I think I'll go for a walk."

Pearl pushed the screen door open and went out on the porch. Except for a lawn mower somewhere in the distance, it was quiet. She walked around the house to the backyard. One of the cats was playing with a bug, jumping around in the tall weeds by the porch.

Pearl walked over to the shed and opened the

squeaky door. She looked back at the house, then stepped inside the shed. She pushed aside the boxes and tools until she found the board in the dirt floor, then lifted it and looked down at the tackle box. The sound of her own heartbeat pounded in her ears. She wiped her sweaty palms on the seat of her shorts and opened the tackle box.

Don't take that, Pearl, said a voice in her head. But she didn't listen. She lifted the bag of coins out of the tackle box, closed the lid, put the board over the hole, pushed the boxes back, and left the shed. She ran through the orchard to the woods, not stopping until she got to the creek. She waded out into the middle. The water was cold and the rocks were slippery. She opened the bag and took out a silver dollar. She glanced behind her, then tossed the coin into the water. It landed with a splash, sending minnows scattering in all directions before settling on the sandy bottom.

Pearl reached into the bag and took another silver dollar. She tossed it into the water. Then another one and another one and another one, until the bag was empty.

She waded out of the creek and climbed the mossy slope that ran beside it. The air was cool and damp. The sound of the running water made Pearl feel sleepy. She looked down at the creek. The silver dollars shimmered in the clear water, like sparkly silver fish. Pearl tossed the canvas bag into the creek, then turned and headed home.

That night, Pearl sat on the floor of her closet, breathing in the mothball smell. She looked at the postcard in her hand—Great Smoky Mountains National Park. Then she wrote:

> *Dear Mama,*
>> *Remember that wrinkled-up old lady in the bed I told you about? Well, she died and now I know I really am invisible like you said I was.*
>>> *Love,*
>>> *Pearl*

17

Moonpie was different now. He jumped off the couch in the morning like he was busting to start the day. Sometimes Pearl stayed in bed and listened to Moon and Ivy in the kitchen, talking a mile a minute about nothing in particular. The weather. The daily special at the diner. John Dee's van in the repair shop.

Pearl wondered how they did that—talking so easy about nothing in particular. Sometimes she practiced, talking to herself in the mirror.

"It's going to be a scorcher today, ain't it?" she'd say to herself, tossing her hair out of her eyes with a casual shake of her head.

"Now who in the world do you think was settin'

off them firecrackers last night?" she'd ask her reflection.

"Looks like the rabbits ate the tops slap off of them onions!" she'd say, jamming her fists into her sides like she was disgusted.

But when it came time for talking in real life, Pearl couldn't seem to get it right. She found herself searching in her head for something to talk about that would sound natural and easy instead of all eat up with bad feelings. She'd start out with something easygoing, but then the next thing she knew she'd be snapping at Ivy or clamming up with Moonpie and feeling like she wanted to kick herself for doing it.

And then the bad feelings would get worse when Moonpie and Ivy let her snapping and clamming up just slide right over them without batting an eye. Pearl had never known two people so hard to fight with.

So that was how Pearl's days started. Moonpie and Ivy chattering away just as cheerful as can be and her coming in there trying to stir things up but not having much luck.

Then one morning something bad happened. Pearl was sitting at the kitchen table, eating pancakes. John Dee was fixing a leaky pipe, lying on the floor with his head up under the sink. Moon sat beside him, handing him wrenches and duct tape.

The radio was on. John Dee's foot tapped on the floor to the tune of a country-western song about somebody in a bar at closing time, wondering where his baby was.

They all jumped when the screen door flew open so hard it banged against the side of the house. Ivy stormed into the kitchen and slammed a rusty metal box onto the kitchen table in front of Pearl. Crash!

Pearl stared at the box. The tackle box from the shed. Her stomach squeezed up and for a minute she thought she was going to throw up.

"Okay, Pearl, start talking," Ivy said.

Pearl couldn't look up. She put her fork down and clutched her hands together in her lap.

"Look at me!" Ivy yelled.

John Dee had come out from under the sink and was standing next to Ivy. He put his arm around her. "Hold on, now, Ivy," he said. "What's going on?"

Ivy stepped away from him and glared down at Pearl. "You got some explaining to do, Pearl," she said.

Pearl looked up. When her eyes met Ivy's, she saw Ruby's face, red and angry and accusing.

"I don't know what you're talking about," she said, trying hard to keep her head up and her eyes on Ivy.

"Don't play games with me, Pearl," Ivy said. She pushed the tackle box toward Pearl so hard it nearly slid right off the table. "Where are them silver dollars?"

"How should I know?" Pearl could feel sweat running down her back. She wanted to run out the back door, across the yard, through the orchard, and on and on as far away from there as she could get. Instead, she sat at the kitchen table and looked down at her pancakes.

Ivy pulled out a chair and sat across from Pearl. She closed her eyes and moved her mouth like she was telling herself to be calm. Then she leaned forward and said, "I want them silver dollars, Pearl. They were my daddy's. I don't know why on this earth you want to hurt me, but taking them silver dollars is the worst kind of hurt. I want them back and I want them back now."

Pearl picked up her fork and threw it clear across the kitchen. It bounced off the toaster with a clang. Then she stood up and glared down at Ivy.

"What makes you so sure it was me that took your precious silver dollars? I ain't the only one in the world, you know." Pearl kicked the leg of the table. "Maybe it was Moonpie that took 'em. You ever think of that?"

They all looked at Moon. He sat on the floor with his mouth hanging open and a look of pure scared on his face.

"Well?" Pearl said. "Why not Moonpie? He knew where them silver dollars were hid. How come you didn't come busting in here and holler at him?"

Ivy turned to Pearl. "Because I know Moon. Known him all his life." Her face softened and she sat back in her chair. "I don't know you, Pearl. Don't know nothing about you, really."

"He ain't even your kin," Pearl said, throwing her arm in Moon's direction. "You put him before your own kin, thinking he's so all-fired perfect?"

John Dee stepped forward and put his hand on Pearl's shoulder. "Moonpie and Ivy—"

Pearl jerked away. "Moonpie and Ivy! Moonpie and Ivy! That's all anybody cares about around here." She stomped toward the door, then whirled back around. "Well, what about me?" she yelled, thumping herself in the chest. Then she turned and ran out of the house, down the steps, across the yard, and through the orchard. Thorns snagged her thin pajamas as she pushed through the weeds. She felt the soft moss under her bare feet on the path in the woods. When she passed the creek, she glanced at the shiny silver dollars, gleaming on the sandy creek bottom, but she kept going until she got to the cemetery. Inside the circle of drooping sunflowers, she dropped to the ground and laid her head on the grave of little Margaret Jane. She pulled her knees up to her chest and put her hands over her face and wished she could sink down into the ground and be a child of heaven like Margaret Jane.

Pearl didn't know how long she had been there when she became aware of a voice. What was the voice saying? She took her hands off her face and listened.

"Pearl . . . sweetheart . . . Pearl . . ." the voice was saying.

Pearl sat up. Ivy was kneeling next to her, rubbing her back, smoothing her hair, touching her cheeks. She tried to pull Pearl toward her, but Pearl put her hands on Ivy's chest and pushed away. "You think I'm bad, don't you?" she said. "Just 'cause of Mama. 'Cause you hate my mama you hate me, too. Ain't that right?"

"I don't hate your mama," Ivy said. "I been trying for thirty years to love her, but I don't hate her."

Ivy reached out and took Pearl's hands in hers. Pearl didn't pull away. "And you?" Ivy said. "Hate you?" She shook her head. "I don't hate you, sweetheart."

"Then how come you love Moonpie so much and not me?"

Ivy looked down at her hands, holding Pearl's, then up at the sky. She let her breath out slowly through her lips, making a soft, whooshing sound. Then she looked at Pearl with such a soft, good-hearted look that Pearl wanted to lay her head down in Ivy's lap.

"These here are my babies," Ivy said, nodding toward the little gravestones beside them. Pearl sat still, not daring to look at Ivy, not wanting Ivy to know that she already knew about Margaret Jane and Rose Marie. Ivy squeezed Pearl's hands a little tighter. "All I ever wanted in this world was a child of my own," she said. "And when God give me these babies and then turned right around and took them away, I thought I'd die. Thought I couldn't possibly take another breath."

Ivy's hands felt warm and soft. Pearl studied her face. The little lines at the corners of her eyes. The sunburned nose. The tiny creases in her eyelids. Pearl didn't want her to stop talking, so she said, "Then what happened?"

"My husband up and left. I reckon my heartbreak was just too much for him. Scared him away, you know?"

Pearl nodded.

"And then Moonpie come along." Ivy smiled and looked out at the cemetery as if she were seeing something that Pearl couldn't see. "He was just a little bitty ole thing. Used to come down off of that hill to play in the orchard, wandering around talking to hisself like he was his own best friend." Ivy looked at Pearl. "I reckon he come to me about the time I needed a best friend myself." She let go of Pearl's hands and ran her fingers over one of the gravestones. "Me and Moon been loving each other for a long time, Pearl."

"What about me?" Pearl said so soft it came out almost a whisper.

Ivy cupped her hands around Pearl's face. "You showed up here and found a place in my heart I didn't even know I had. But you *got* a mama, Pearl. You belong with her, not me. That don't mean I don't love you. It just means that's the way the world works and we got to live with it."

"But she left me," Pearl said. "If I belong with her, then she don't know it."

"Ruby's a puzzle, that's for sure." Ivy winked at Pearl. "But I bet she says the same thing about me, don't she?"

Pearl shook her head. "She don't say nothing about you. Except how you're a good cook and all."

Ivy chuckled. "I know I shouldn't say so many bad things about your mama, Pearl, but I can't help it. The only thing predictable about Ruby is that she's gonna mess things up for me. I never know when or how, but sure as shootin' it's gonna happen."

Pearl nodded. She could sure understand that. But right now she had a bigger worry eating at her.

"If she don't want me and you don't want me, then what am I going to do?" Pearl said. She felt the tears running down her cheeks. Watched them drop onto her lap. She waited for Ivy to say, "But your mama does want you" or "But I do want you," but she didn't say either of those things. She pointed to the dried, brown sunflowers circling the graves and said, "See them sunflowers?"

Pearl nodded.

"I plant them wherever I need to find hope."

"How come?"

" 'Cause they're like a sign. A sign of hope for something new and good. You know, it's really a miracle when you think about it. How you have this tiny little seed and then before long you got this big, beautiful flower. And then right in the middle of that flower are more seeds waiting to start all over again." She looked up at the sunflowers. "I see them flowers and I know that even though they're gonna die, them seeds are there—like a sign. You know, a sign that more flowers will come along." She put her arm around Pearl. "A sign of hope. See what I mean?"

"Why'd you plant them in this graveyard?" Pearl said. "Are you hoping for more babies?"

Ivy shook her head and rubbed the gravestone beside her. "I gave up hope of ever having babies a long time ago," she said. "I guess I just need to come here and be with my babies and not get eat up with sad. I

134

need to have hope—and I do. I lost my babies, but I still got hope for happiness."

"Not me," Pearl said.

"Maybe you're just not looking in the right place," Ivy said.

They sat close together, their hands on each other's knees. Rain began to fall, soft and quiet. Pearl looked up at the sunflowers bowing over their heads. "Maybe," she said.

18

Later that day, Moon helped Pearl collect the silver dollars from the creek. A fine, drizzly rain fell. Leaves hung wet and heavy from the trees, dripping rainwater on their heads as they searched the creek bottom. They worked in silence, pushing aside sand and leaves and rocks with their bare feet. When they came across a silver dollar, they dropped it into the pillowcase Ivy had given Pearl to hold the wet, dirty coins.

Every now and then Pearl glanced at Moon. His cantaloupe hair hung in wet clumps over his eyes. He moved slowly, peering through the clear water in total concentration. Pearl was still fascinated by the whiteness of his skin. The scattering of pale freckles. The tiny veins showing through the side of his neck. And those gold eyelashes blinking slowly over his pale, spooky eyes.

Pearl spotted a coin nestled in a bed of rotten leaves. She picked it up, wiped it on the seat of her shorts, and dropped it into the pillowcase.

"How come you're being so nice to me?" she said.

Moon lifted his head and looked at Pearl. "What?"

"I said, how come you're being so nice to me?"

"I ain't being nice to you." His nearly invisible eyebrows squeezed together. "I mean, not on purpose. I mean, I ain't *trying* to be nice, I'm just . . ."

"I bet Ivy told you to be nice to me."

Moon stared at Pearl. He scratched a mosquito bite on his leg, then waded out of the creek and sat on the mossy bank. "Why would she do that?" he said.

"So you wouldn't be mean to me."

"Why would I be mean to you?"

Pearl threw her hands up. The coins rattled in the pillowcase. " 'Cause of what I done! With the silver dollars." Her voice came out high and squeaky.

Pearl waded out of the creek, sloshing water onto Moonpie. She sat beside him and stared at him with her lips set tight.

"How come you don't even care what anybody does to you?" she said.

"I care."

"Must not."

"Why do you think that?"

" 'Cause you ain't even acting mad about these silver dollars," Pearl said, jiggling the pillowcase near Moon's face. "Shoot, you don't even get it . . . why I took 'em and all. Why I told Ivy it might've been you that took 'em."

"Why did you?"

Pearl shook her head. Her hair was damp and frizzy. She wiped water out of her eyes and studied Moon's face. "So nobody would like you anymore," she said.

"Oh," he said, wiggling his toes on the wet moss. "I thought you did it so nobody would like *you*."

Pearl stared at Moon. What was he talking about?

"You're crazy, then," she said. "I don't have to do *nothing* to make people not like me. All I got to do is breathe."

Moon tossed a stick into the creek. "Then maybe you should try doing something to make people *like* you," he said.

Then he stood up, wiped mud off the seat of his shorts, and left.

When Pearl gave Ivy the soggy pillowcase and said, "We found every one of 'em," Ivy hugged her. A long, quiet, hair-stroking hug. Pearl closed her eyes and

breathed in Ivy's smell. Talcum powder and cinnamon.

"Now," Ivy said. "Why don't I get myself in to the
diner so we can catch a movie later. How would that
be?"

"That'd be good," Pearl said.

"John Dee's taking Moon into town to get some pa-
perwork filled out with that social worker. I expect
they'll be home by dinnertime."

"Okay."

Ivy took her apron off and reached for her purse.
"Would you put those back out there in the shed?" she
said, nodding toward the silver dollars on the kitchen
counter.

"Yes, ma'am."

Ivy smiled, then turned and headed toward the
front door.

"Ivy," Pearl called.

Ivy stopped and turned around, holding the screen
door open. Pearl struggled to keep from looking down
at the floor.

"I'm sorry," she said. "About the silver dollars, I
mean."

Ivy flapped her hand at Pearl. "Aw, now," she said.
"See you tonight."

"Ivy," Pearl called from the porch just as Ivy
reached the car.

Ivy turned and waited.

"If you wanted somebody to like you," Pearl said, "what would you do?"

"Well, I reckon I'd just be myself."

"But what if you already tried that and it didn't work?"

Ivy opened the car door and climbed inside. "You sure ask some hard questions, my little Pearl." She shut the door and rolled down the window. "I'm flattered you think I'm that smart, but the truth of the matter is I got no answers for them hard questions."

Pearl watched Ivy's car disappear down the gravel road. The rain had stopped but the sky was still gray and gloomy.

Pearl went back to her bedroom and took the shoebox off the closet shelf. She took out the ballet shoe necklace and went across the hall to Ivy's room. She opened Ivy's jewelry box and watched the little ballerina twirl around. Then she dropped the necklace inside and closed the lid. When she looked up, she saw herself in the mirror over the dresser and was surprised to see how much she looked like Ruby. Same thin lips. Same frowning gray eyes.

She went back to her room and sat on the bed, looking down at the yellow-bird music box nestled among the postcards in the shoebox. She lifted the bird out and wound it up. Then she held it up in the palm of her hand, watching the bird turn around and around on its nest of flowers. She pretended she was little Ruby, holding that very same bird, listening to that very same tune. "When I grow up, little bird," she said, "I'm going to have me a girl named Pearl and I'm going to think she's a gem of the world and she ain't never going to be invisible and I ain't never going to leave her no matter what."

Then Pearl tucked the music box under her T-shirt and left the house. She hurried up the hill to Moon's house. Skeeter wagged his tail when he saw her coming.

"Hey, there, Skeeter boy," she said, giving the old dog a pat on the head.

She went inside. The house was dark and damp and smelled like mildew. Pearl quickly placed the bird on the shelf over the bed, left the house, patted Skeeter one more time, then ran down the hill toward Ivy's.

That night, Pearl studied a postcard. Whitewater Falls. She remembered being there with Ruby one time. They had sat in the car and read the sign that told how the top of the waterfall was in North Carolina and the bottom was in South Carolina. They had eaten lunch on the curb, listening to the roar of the water behind them. Pearl still remembered how the bees had swarmed around her jelly sandwich. How she had sung "Jesus Loves Me" about a hundred times while Ruby drank vodka and orange juice from a soda bottle. Then Ruby had slept in the backseat of the car until long after dark and Pearl had locked the car doors so bears wouldn't eat them.

Pearl turned the postcard over and wrote:

Dear Mama,
When you put that yellow bird
music box back after you stole it,
did people start liking you? I hope
the answer is yes, because I don't
know what else to do.
Love,
Pearl

19

"I wonder if four dozen is enough," Ivy said, scooping the last of the hermit cookies onto a plate to cool.

Pearl had no idea if four dozen was enough, but she tried to look like she was seriously considering the question.

"Let's see," Ivy said, narrowing her eyes and looking up at the ceiling. "I got about three dozen oatmeal cookies, and some of them lemon bars . . ."

"And some of them cookies with the kisses in the middle," Moonpie said.

Ivy smiled and ruffled Moon's hair. "And some of them cookies with the kisses in the middle. I reckon that oughtta do it. John Dee thinks I should make chili, but I think it's too hot. What do y'all think?"

"I never heard of having chili at a wedding," Pearl said. "And what about a wedding cake? Ain't you even going to have a wedding cake?"

"Genevieve might make a sheet cake."

Pearl thought a sheet cake was a sorry excuse for a wedding cake, but she decided not to say it.

"I know!" Ivy snapped her fingers. "Catfish! We could fry up some catfish and hush puppies."

"Yeah!" Moon said. "That'd be good."

Ivy untied her apron and draped it over the back of a chair.

"It's too dern hot in here," she said. "Let's go sit on the porch before the mosquitoes come out."

Pearl loved sitting on the porch this time of day— that slow, quiet time between daylight and dark. Ivy sat in an aluminum lawn chair. Pearl and Moon sat on the steps. A faint ripple of a breeze drifted over them. Ivy waved a paper fan in front of her face.

When Pearl heard the crunch of the gravel on the road, she leaned forward and looked. Way off down the road, a car bounced along toward them. Too fast. Dust and gravel flying. The car squeaked and groaned with every bounce.

All three of them watched. Pearl and Moonpie and

Ivy. Craning their necks and squinting their eyes trying to see better. The car squeaked and bounced its way closer.

And then Pearl's stomach dropped clear down to her feet and her eyes burned and her hands gripped her knees and her thoughts raced around like a bee in a mason jar.

Ivy stood up, letting her fan fall to the floor. She watched the car. Moonpie watched the car. Pearl watched the car.

Chickens squawked and disappeared around the side of the house as the car stopped abruptly in the driveway with one final crunch of gravel.

The car door opened with a squeak and Ruby jumped out with her arms spread wide and called, "Where's my Pearlie May?"

Nobody moved. Pearl could hear Ivy breathing behind her.

Ruby put her hands on her hips. Her hair was redder, longer, curlier than Pearl remembered. She wore a short denim skirt. Her freckled legs looked skinnier. She was barefoot. Pearl looked down at Ruby's toenails. Cranberry red. Ruby's favorite color from her nail polish collection.

"Well?" Ruby said, coming toward them.

"Hey, Ruby," Ivy said.

Ruby's lips were smiling but her eyes weren't. She held her palms up and lifted her shoulders. "Well?" she said again.

Still nobody moved. Pearl closed her eyes. She wondered if Ruby would still be there when she opened them. She opened them. Ruby was still there.

"Okay, Pearlie May," she said. "Listen to this. Remember how you used to have that puzzle that was a map of the United States and how you used to take it apart and put it together and take it apart and put it together till you liked to run me wild? And then one time there was a piece missing? Remember that?"

Pearl nodded. Ivy cleared her throat and said, "Ruby . . ."

"Well," Ruby went on, "you remember how you carried on about that piece?" She chuckled. "Lord, I thought you were gonna tear that house apart looking for that dern little ole puzzle piece. Remember?"

Pearl nodded again.

Ruby moved closer to Pearl. Shalimar. Pearl's throat felt dry and tight, like she couldn't swallow.

"Do you remember what state that was?" Ruby said, cocking her head at Pearl.

"Arizona," Pearl said.

"Yes!" Ruby squealed, clapping her hands together.

146

"That's where we're going. Arizona!" She waited, but Pearl just stared down at those cranberry red toenails. Ruby's mouth twitched slightly. "Phoenix, Arizona," she said. "How about *that?*"

Ruby's mouth twitched again when nobody said anything. "Oh, wait," she said, holding up a finger. "Guess what else?" She ran to the car and came back with a Wal-Mart bag. She reached in and took out a portable CD player. "Just like I promised," she said.

Just like she promised? Pearl looked Ruby square in the face for the first time since the bouncing, squeaking car had stopped in the driveway and Ruby had jumped out.

"What?" Ruby said, her mouth set in that hard smile, her eyes darting from Ivy to Pearl. Then her smile disappeared and she went back to the car and yanked a pack of cigarettes off the dashboard. She pushed past all three of them and went in the house. The screen door slammed and Pearl jumped and her heart squeezed up tight in her chest.

Pearl sat motionless, staring straight ahead but not seeing anything. She felt Ivy's hand on the top of her head. Heard Ivy go into the house. Moonpie stirred beside her, but didn't get up.

Angry voices came from inside the house. Ruby's, then Ivy's, then Ruby's. Pearl had that confusing feel-

147

ing again. That feeling of wanting something and not wanting something at the same time. She wanted to know what those angry voices were saying. But at the same time, she didn't. Still, she couldn't stop some of the angry words from floating out the screen door and hovering around her. She couldn't seem to fit the words together. They were just words. Child. Crazy. Daughter. Pearl. Mother. And then one great big, loud, "Mind your own damn business."

"Let's go up and see Skeeter," Pearl said.

It was dark by the time Pearl and Moon got back to Ivy's. As they crossed the backyard, Pearl could see Ruby in the glow of the porch light. She was sitting on the back steps smoking. When she saw Pearl, she stood up and said, "Pack your things. We're leaving."

So she did. Stuffed her T-shirts and shorts and underwear and pajamas into her ratty old duffel bag. Fished her dirty socks and sneakers from under the bed. Grabbed her toothbrush from beside the bathroom sink. Then she stood on tiptoe and reached for her shoebox on the closet shelf. She searched through the postcards until she found the right one. Georgia peaches.

She turned it over and wrote:

Dear Ivy,

Thank you.

Love,

Pearl

She propped the postcard up on her pillow, turned out the light, and left the room.

The icy silence in the house felt stifling. Like it was sucking the air out. Pearl carried her duffel bag and shoebox outside. Ruby waited by the car. Moonpie and Ivy stood on the porch.

Pearl looked at Ivy. "It was nice meeting you," she said in a tiny little voice that didn't sound like hers.

Ivy grabbed Pearl's shoulders and pulled her close. She pressed Pearl's cheek against her chest. Then she kissed the top of Pearl's head. "Wait here," she said. "I'll be right back."

Pearl and Moon waited on the porch. Moths circled the dusty bulb overhead. Ruby got in the car and slammed the door shut. She lit a cigarette and blew the smoke out the open window.

Ivy came back out on the porch and handed Pearl a brown envelope.

"You take care, sweetheart, okay?" she said.

Pearl hung her head and said, "Okay." She stopped to put the envelope in her shoebox, then gathered her things and went out to the car. Moonpie and Ivy followed her.

The car door squeaked when Pearl opened it. She climbed in and shut the door behind her. She rolled down the window and looked up at Moonpie and Ivy. Ivy kept dabbing at her eyes. Moonpie shuffled his feet around in the dirt.

Ruby started the car with a roar and jerked the gearshift into reverse. The tires spun briefly in the gravel before the car lunged backward out of the driveway. Moon ran to the road and called out, "I like you, Pearl."

Pearl turned and looked out the rear window as the car headed up the road away from Ivy's. Moonpie and Ivy stood in the road with their arms around each other. They grew smaller and smaller in the red glow of the taillights—and then they disappeared.

Pearl turned back around and looked out the window at the darkness. Ruby was jabbering on about Arizona and cowboys and Mexican food, but Pearl let her thoughts push Ruby's words away. She thought about Moonpie and Ivy and how they fit together so natural. She thought about how her whole life had been a big jumble of mixed-up craziness. And then she'd had this one little taste of the normal side of life, of people treating each other good and being deserving of love, and she hadn't belonged. Had felt wrong and out of place. A fish out of water, flopping around trying to be normal, too. She knew she hadn't been very good at normal living, but she thought maybe she could get the hang of it if she had another chance.

When they left the bumpy gravel road and turned onto the main highway, Pearl remembered the brown envelope. She took it out of the shoebox and looked inside. Sunflower seeds. And nestled down among the seeds was the ballet shoe necklace and a folded scrap of paper. Pearl lifted the necklace out and put it over her head. She dropped the little ballet shoes down inside her shirt and pressed her hand against them.

Then she took a sunflower seed from the envelope and put it in her mouth. She bit into it, tasting the gritty earthiness of it. She chewed and chewed and then she swallowed, because that's where she needed to find hope. Inside herself.

She opened the scrap of paper and squinted at it in the glow of the dashboard lights. "Ivy Patterson" was scrawled in big, hurried letters. Underneath, circled in red, was a phone number. Pearl closed her eyes and said the numbers in her head again and again and again.

She put the envelope back in the shoebox. Ruby droned on and on.

"Wait till you see . . .

"You're gonna love . . .

"I was thinking we could . . ."

But Pearl wasn't listening. She hugged the shoe-box, thinking maybe she could already feel that hope starting to grow inside her. Then she whispered Ivy's phone number over and over while she stared out at the dark road ahead.